exposed:
LAID BARE

exposed:
LAID BARE

Amazon Bestselling Author

S.R. GREY

Exposed: Laid Bare (Laid Bare #1)
Copyright © 2014 by S.R. Grey

ISBN-10: 0986156515
ISBN-13: 978-0-9861565-1-9

Editing: Hot Tree Editing
Cover Design: Arijana Karčić, Cover It!
Interior design and rormatting by

E.M.
TIPPETTS
BOOK DESIGNS

www.emtippettsbookdesigns.com

Other Books by
S.R. GREY

A Harbour Falls Mystery trilogy

Harbour Falls
Willow Point
Wickingham Way

Judge Me Not trilogy

I Stand Before You
Never Doubt Me
Just Let Me Love You

Inevitability Duology

Inevitable Detour
Inevitable Circumstances (coming May 2015)

chapter ONE

*J*ust as I was taking in a sweeping gaze of the most magnificent Christmas party I'd ever attended, someone snuck up behind me and whispered in my ear, "You are such a little bitch, Dahlia."

"Veronica," I huffed, annoyed.

I tried to spin around to confront my verbal assailant—who also happened to be my best friend and cousin who delighted in driving me crazy—but before I could get my bearings, Veronica's delicate, slender fingers slid over my eyes.

Everything went black, but the smells and sounds of the holidays were still all around me. Eggnog and cinnamon scents punctuated the air, and the comforting lull of classic holiday tunes filled my ears.

But with my sight obscured as it was, there would be no more gazing at the yards and yards of multi-colored, twinkling lights draped from the raw wood beam rafters above me, and no more admiring the sparkling, decorated fifteen-foot fir in the far corner of the large banquet hall the party was being held in.

Prior to Veronica's interruption, I'd been mesmerized by the tree with its shiny glass ornaments and bright lights adorning the branches. I found it amazing how the holiday glow made all the beautiful party guests look even more dazzling. Glamorous and sophisticated, all dressed in their holiday party finest and milling around, drinking too much champagne, having too much fun. But the glitz and glamour were momentarily hidden from me, thanks to Veronica's hand over my eyes.

"Are you done," I inquired. I made my tone sound miffed, but I wasn't, not really.

"No, and don't look now," she replied from behind me, hand still in place.

"As if I could," I interjected as I shifted from one way-too-high stiletto heel to the other. "So, why am I a bitch?" I continued. "And why in God's name are you still covering my eyes?"

"First, you're not really a bitch," Veronica replied apologetically. "And secondly, the answer to your other question, my dear, just walked in the door."

Aha! Her answer, not to mention her tone, meant one thing and one thing only — *he* was here.

Oh, boy.

I pushed Veronica's hand away, blinked twice, and peered through the crowd. It wasn't hard to spot the man I sought, not with his commanding height and his room-filling presence. He radiated confidence and outshined even the loveliest of guests. With his coal-black hair and, seemingly, even darker eyes, combined with a lithe body and the best bone structure I'd ever seen on a man, Lucien Chambers was quite the male specimen. Still, I could barely believe what was so clearly in front of me — Mr. Chambers, guest of honor at this year's Lucent Magazine bigwig holiday party, had actually taken it upon himself to grace everyone with his presence.

Interesting.

Lucien, entrepreneur, millionaire at age twenty-four — *multi*-millionaire three years later — was successful and loaded. And at age twenty-nine, as of last month, he'd been declared Chicago's most eligible bachelor.

Well, he definitely deserved the title. Lucien was rich, stunning to look at, and available. I'd previously read that he dated frequently — usually beautiful models, of course—but he'd never gotten married. Perhaps he'd just never found the right one.

No surprise there. I imagined a man such as Lucien would possess rather discerning tastes.

Glancing over at my beautiful cousin, I thought about how Veronica would have been a good match for Lucien. With platinum blonde hair that flowed to her waist, a killer body, and icy blue eyes, she was almost as stunning as Lucien...almost. Oh well. Too bad she was engaged.

I returned my attention back to the situation at hand, murmuring, "Hmm, this *is* unusual."

"What?" I could feel Veronica's cool blue eyes on me, assessing.

"Nobody thought Mr. Chambers would put in an appearance tonight, given his reclusive nature."

"Well, he's here," she replied matter-of-factly.

Yes, he sure was. And—uh-oh—he was currently walking my way.

"Shit," I hissed rather loudly.

Veronica paid me no heed, though. She was too busy leaning into me and whispering in my ear, "Oh, Dahl, just look at him. That man is so damn sexy."

"I am looking," I said.

And, oh, was I ever. It was almost impossible not to stare, as Lucien was one smoking hot man. And tonight he looked especially magnificent in his dark gray suit, the ritzy fabric allowing his body to move elegantly and fluidly.

"Wow," I sighed. "He is impressive, right?"

"For sure," Veronica murmured.

There was something more about the man, though, something beyond his great looks that made him so appealing. Lucien was a man with great confidence.

Conversely, I was the exact opposite — a woman with very little confidence.

So, of course, as he neared me, I spun around and grabbed up Veronica's hand. "Quick," I said, "let's get out of here."

"What? Why? Are you crazy?" was Veronica's certainly understandable response. She tried to twist away, but I kept my hold firm.

"Come on," I urged once more, this time tugging for effect. "Please, V."

Veronica held steady, but her voice turned soft and understanding when she said, "Why don't you want to meet him tonight, Dahlia? You'll be working with the man soon enough."

"That's exactly why I don't want to meet him," I replied.

I tugged Veronica's arm again to get her moving, and added, "You know my rules."

Finally, *that* got her moving. And just in time, as Lucien was gaining ground.

"Okay, okay," Veronica said as I turned us away at the same second Lucien's searing gaze connected with mine.

Too late, I'm outta here, my parting glance conveyed.

As I dragged my cousin in the direction of the rest rooms — surely a safe spot — she murmured under her breath, "How could I have forgotten about you and your weird idiosyncrasies?"

Okay, yes, she had a point. I was a little weird about my work, quirky even, but my weirdness kept my creativity at play. I am a photographer, you see, and a damn good one. Not meeting my subjects before taking their picture is an integral part of my creative process. I prefer to go in to photo shoots cold. That way I learn my subject as I work. It makes for a better outcome, and I have the award-winning photographs to prove it.

"Come on," I hurried my cousin along, toward an alcove with a tastefully small, gold plate engraved with the word *Ladies*.

"Calm down," she said. "He's not following us now. He stopped to talk with someone."

"He may catch up," I replied, worried.

"Oh, Dahlia…" Veronica shook her head.

She was sweet to indulge me, but she understood my idiosyncrasies. Veronica is a photographer too, and has her own quirks to contend with. The two of us freelance around the city. My cousin is good, very talented, but I am better. Not to brag, it just is what it is. That's why I was awarded the prestigious gig of shooting Lucien Chambers the day after Christmas.

Interacting with him in seven more days would be soon enough. I'd have time to build up my courage by then and, hopefully, not make a fool of myself. Photographing Mr. Chambers—for a piece Lucent Magazine was running on him and his many business successes—had the power to make or break my career. He gave so few interviews and rarely allowed himself to be photographed, so this was a coup. The only reason he agreed to this news piece was because he'd recently bought a stake in the magazine.

Needless to say, I was nervous as hell. I could not screw up this job.

"I still can't believe you're passing up the chance to meet Lucien Chambers," Veronica mused out loud. "Surely, a little preview won't mess with your wacky ways."

"I'll meet him next week at the shoot," I maintained, keeping Veronica moving through the crowd and away from Mr. Eligible Bachelor.

Finally, we reached the ladies room. I hurried in, Veronica in tow, and closed the door behind us.

Turning to me, Veronica rolled her eyes. "Well, you're safe now. I doubt he'll dare step in here." She gestured around at all the feminine décor in the ornate facility. "There is way too much estrogen in this room for any man."

"I think you're right," I agreed, smiling at all the flowery and frilly detail everywhere.

Stepping over to one of the many floor-to-ceiling mirrors on the walls, I let out a sigh of relief.

But when I took in my reflection—seeing only disheveled auburn hair and green eyes with lashes in dire need of a mascara touch-up—I murmured dejectedly, "Damn, I'm glad he didn't catch up to us. Ugh. Look at me, Veronica, I'm a mess."

"Oh, you're fine," she said.

But, quietly, after a beat, I disagreed and added, "No wonder I've never had a boyfriend."

My cousin stepped over to me and leaned her head against my shoulder. Lovingly, she adjusted the ruby red spaghetti strap of my silk dress. "You look beautiful, as always, Dahl. Any man would be lucky to have you."

"Maybe," I mused, leaning my head to hers. "Too bad no man wants me."

"That's not true."

"Yeah, it kind of is."

Veronica sighed. "You're gorgeous, hon, but you are a little too picky for your own good."

Now, it was my turn to sigh, because, sadly, she was correct. I was mighty choosy. A few dates, a couple of vanilla kisses. That was my experience in the areas of love, lust, and men. And it was all because my standards were pretty much unattainable.

Not that I had any standards defined, not exactly. Still, it was as if there was this little voice in my head urging me to wait.

I was waiting for something...or someone. I just didn't know which one. In any case, I sure hoped that that something — or someone — happened soon.

Mostly because being a virgin at the age of twenty-six was beginning to feel downright embarrassing.

chapter
TWO

I had successfully avoided Lucien at the Christmas party, but he was still on my mind.

Over the next few days, I busied myself with researching him, as per my process. Despite the fact I didn't like to meet my future subjects, I did enjoy thoroughly researching them. Unfortunately, I was finding it surprisingly difficult to come up with much of anything on the elusive Lucien Chambers. Sure, I had all his basic stats—age, occupation, businesses he owned—but I needed to delve deeper. I wanted to find more info regarding Lucien's early years. That task, however, was proving to be quite a feat.

Odd.

From the scant articles I was able to dig up I

learned Lucien was born to a Spanish mother and an English father. He had no siblings, and his parents still lived in his hometown of London. They were wealthy — very wealthy — people. Business moguls just like Lucien.

And that was it.

Those few basic facts were all I could find on the Chambers family, leading me to conclude Lucien's parents were just as reclusive and secretive as their son.

After a final attempt at digging, where I wished I was more of a sleuth like Veronica, I managed to stumble across one article that provided me with slightly more detail on Lucien. It seemed at the age of eighteen, the young Mr. Chambers was determined to make it on his own terms. Consequently, he immigrated to the United States, started an import-export business, and ended up making a name for himself rather rapidly.

The rest of that story I knew. Lucien was involved in all sorts of businesses — manufacturing, retail, and his most recent foray into magazine publishing. Lucent magazine, formerly known as Chicago Now!, had been failing miserably until Lucien stepped in. He changed the name and, over the course of a few months, turned the magazine around. It was a glossy must-have these days.

Fascinating, I thought. It seemed everything Lucien Chambers touched turned to gold.

The other thing I found bizarre was that there were so few photographs of him. Lucien truly seemed to abhor the spotlight, despite the fact he was so incredibly photogenic.

The photos I could find of him — photographs that appeared to be re-circulated and used over and over again — were nothing short of stunning.

So, wow, what a coup it was for me that I was actually going to be photographing Lucien…and in only two days.

The only thing left was to finalize the logistics.

Picking up my cell phone, I called my agent, Shannon. She had secured the gig for me, and she was in charge of the details.

"Dahlia?" she said as she answered on the second ring. "Hold on a sec, dear."

"Okay," I replied

She was always putting me on hold, so I was used to it. I heard her mumble something to someone in the background, and then she got back to me.

"I'm glad you called," she began. "I was actually about to call you."

"Oh?"

"Yes. I heard from Mr. Chamber's people and have directions to the shoot for you."

"Great." I grabbed up a pen and paper. "Okay, I'm ready."

As I jotted down the road names and turns I'd need to make, I realized I was writing out directions that would lead me to an area north of Chicago. And that made no sense.

"Wait," I interrupted, dropping the pen. "I'm not familiar with any studios up in that area."

Having worked in Chicago for quite some time, I knew every photography studio in a hundred mile radius of the town, and this address didn't ring a single bell.

Shannon cleared her throat. "Uh, Mr. Chambers didn't like the studio idea."

"Oh, he didn't?" I let out an odd little laugh. Nervous or annoyed, I couldn't be sure.

"No," Shannon continued. "And he specifically requested *this* location as an alternative."

"Okay." I spoke slowly and shrugged as I picked up the pen I'd dropped to the desk. "So, where am I going? Where does Mr. Chambers want the shoot to take place?"

"At his house," Shannon replied.

The day after Christmas, I discovered Lucien Chambers' house was hardly just a house. It was more like a freaking mansion.

Driving through the gilt-edged gates and up along the long driveway in my little hybrid economy car made me feel small and insignificant. I couldn't help it, as the driveway looked like a long, black asphalt tongue, and I half-expected it to roll up and spit me back out onto the street, screaming at me the whole way, "You don't belong here! Get out!"

Obviously, though, that did not happen.

Despite my overactive imagination, I made it without incident to the entrance of Lucien's Tudor mansion. But before I had the chance to turn off the ignition, a valet appeared, seemingly out of nowhere, and strode up to the car.

Where had he come from?

The trim, gray-haired man motioned for me to roll down my window, and I murmured a startled, "Oh," as I obliged him.

"Welcome, Miss Vaughn," he said with a tip of his fuzzy charcoal beret.

With the window glass lowered, a bitter breeze

blew in.

Ignoring the cold, I replied, "I'm sorry, sir, that I didn't see you right away. Were you behind those bushes?"

I nodded to a long, bare hedgerow, but he gave me no response. Instead, he smiled kindly.

I blew out a breath, and started to open the car door. Mr. Valet quickly took over, swinging the door wide, and saying, "Do hurry, Miss Vaughn, Mr. Chambers doesn't like to be kept waiting."

"I bet," I murmured under my breath as I gathered up my camera cases. When I got out of the car my body began to shiver.

Noting the setting, low-in-the-sky winter sun, and in an awkward attempt to make conversation, I remarked, "Wow, the days sure are short this time of year, aren't they?"

The valet nodded. "Yes, miss, indeed they are." He then slid into the driver's seat of my car, and continued, "Mr. Chambers is waiting inside for you. He requested that you proceed to the front door and knock once."

I supposed that was my cue to go, so I gave the valet a small wave, hoisted my camera bags high on my shoulder, and walked away.

The wind roared and the trees creaked as I hurried

across the driveway to the wide concrete steps leading up to the mansion. With a sudden, inexplicable chill that came from within, I reached the base of the steps and peered upward.

With trepidation, I started my ascent, and with every step I took it seemed the air grew colder and colder. The winds got in on the act, too, roaring and whistling through the bare trees. By the time I reached the massive, dark wood double doors at the top of the steps, my teeth were chattering.

"Shit, I'm freezing," I bit out.

Tugging at the lapels of my heavy woolen coat made not a bit of difference, so I resorted to wrapping my arms around myself and bouncing up and down on my toes. The camera bags tapped at my right hip over and over, not unlike a nudging warning to flee.

But something made me stay, some inexplicable feeling.

I had on sexy, high-heeled black boots and a thin wrap dress in a festive holiday green that matched my eyes. The boots were okay, but the silky fabric of the dress was doing nothing to keep the icy air from nipping at my bare skin beneath. I'd foregone undergarments for this visit, which was very unlike me, and that omission was currently contributing to my freezing my ass off.

"What were you thinking?" I asked myself.

But I knew the answer — I wanted to feel sexy. Though, now, I couldn't for the life of me remember why. Perhaps my choice of attire was due to my reaction as I'd continued to research Lucien. Not being able to find much on the man made him mysterious and appealing. Not to mention, his great looks were a heady turn-on, even for a virginal girl like me.

I stared at the heavy iron knockers — roaring lion's heads on each of the two doors — for what felt like an eternity. I supposed I was mesmerized by their strangeness. In fact, the whole place was kind of strange. Valets appearing out of thin air, plummeting temperatures, howling winds. And now the lion-head door knockers were appearing almost life-like, which was ridiculous since they were made of iron. So why, then, did it feel as if their eyes were watching me, assessing me?

"You are losing it," I muttered to myself.

And that was the point where I began questioning the wisdom of coming to this house alone. Something felt off. The icy wind that continued to whip around me did nothing to soothe these unsettled feelings. But, for whatever reason, I also felt compelled to stay, to see how this evening with Lucien might play out.

"Be brave," I whispered for encouragement as I

reached for the iron ring attached to the lion-head on the right.

And then, suddenly, when my fingers wrapped around the iron knocker, I felt inexplicably soothed.

"This place is bizarre," I said out loud as I commenced knocking.

Several minutes passed, and within that time, everything grew quiet. The property was secluded, yes, but even the branches on the acres and acres of surrounding trees seemed to stop creaking. They had been so loud earlier, as had the now-quieted whipping wind.

Maybe I should go…

But just as I was about to turn tail and leave, Lucien Chambers opened the door. "Miss Vaughn." He had the slightest British accent. "Please do come in."

He smiled at me, and he looked so amazing, so appealing. I couldn't even move a muscle at first. I stood there and stared, taking in his casual attire of dark pants and a cream-colored, cashmere sweater, which contrasted beautifully with his coal black hair.

Interestingly, I noticed Lucien had on no shoes or socks. Even so, he seemed not one bit bothered by the cold.

But I spent no time dwelling on those oddities.

Instead, I concentrated on Lucien's wide shoulders, the breadth of his chest, and the appealing way his torso tapered at his waist. His sweater looked so soft against his hard frame, and I longed to reach out and touch him, to feel how the softness of the sweater contrasted with Lucien's hard-looking chest.

Of course, I refrained from making any such bold move. Even so, when I peered up at Lucien from beneath my lashes, it was as if he knew what I was thinking.

The side of his luscious mouth curved up into a knowing smile, and I became flustered, my gaze skittering away.

God, he is angelically beautiful, I thought.

But devilishly onto you, I reluctantly added.

I questioned whether Lucien was really human, seeing into my head as I knew he was. But then I thought, *How ridiculous.*

"Something wrong, Miss Vaughn," Lucien asked, his dark, penetrating eyes assessing me for my reaction when I glanced up.

"No, nothing is wrong," I squeaked. Clearing my throat, I added in what I hoped was a more level voice, "I was just thinking we should get started with the session. It's getting late."

"Of course, Miss Vaughn. Your wish is my

command." Smirking, he stepped aside and motioned for me to come in.

I moved forward, carefully, so as not to touch him. Not that I didn't trust Lucien. I didn't trust myself. I was thinking and feeling far too many strange things, like how I suddenly wanted him in a way I'd never known a man.

Once in the house, Lucien beckoned me to follow him. He led me through an entry corridor with frosted side windows, and then in to a grand, high-ceilinged hall.

I set my camera bags down on the marble floor, and, in awe, spun around once. "Wow," I gushed. "Your home is beautiful."

Opulence, opulence, everywhere I turned. Apart from the marble floor, there was a crystal chandelier hanging from the ceiling and expensive-looking artwork on the walls.

Post-appraisal, I murmured, "Quite impressive, Mr. Chambers."

"Thank you," Lucien replied. He looked down in an almost humble sort of way. His reaction made him oddly endearing, like he was exposing a vulnerability to me.

Clearing my throat (and my head), I murmured, "Mr. Chambers, we really should get started."

"Please, just call me Lucien," Lucien said. "Mr. Chambers sounds so stuffy."

"Okay." I smiled at him. "But only if you agree to call me by my first name, as well."

"Certainly," he replied charmingly, "I think we have ourselves a deal, Dahlia."

I liked the way my first name rolled off his tongue. It was as if he were tasting every letter, as well as tasting *me*.

"Uh…" I glanced around.

Suddenly, I was feeling incredibly warm.

"May I take your coat?" Lucien asked presciently.

"Yes, yes." I shrugged out of the sleeves, but then stopped, coat partway off, front gaping open. "Hey, don't you have servants to do this sort of thing," I wondered out loud.

He chuckled, despite my forwardness…or maybe because of it.

"I've given everyone the evening off tonight," he explained. "So we could have some privacy."

"Oh."

His dark eyes slid to my chest, and I realized my nipples had hardened, the pointed peaks pressing through the thin material of my dress. I hurriedly removed my coat the rest of the way and folded it over so I could place it in front of my traitorous chest.

Damn this dress. Why had I chosen it? My breasts weren't huge, but they were too big to be prancing around braless in something so flimsy.

What had I been thinking?

If I were to be honest, I knew the answer. I wanted Lucien's attention. I wanted him to feel attracted to me, just as I felt attracted to him.

Well, if my intent had been to capture Lucien's male attention, it was working. He was trying to be coy, but I could see he was checking out what he could see of my somewhat, but not fully, covered cleavage.

"Here." He reached for my coat. "I'll hang that up for you."

I handed him my coat, which provided him an opportunity to see everything I'd been hiding. And look he did. Damn, did he ever. His dark eyes soaked me in hungrily, moving shamelessly from my chest to the ample swell of my hips.

"You're a very beautiful woman," Lucien said in a rough voice. "But you know that, Dahlia, don't you?"

I shook my head. "Actually, I don't think that way about myself at all. But thank you for saying so, Lucien."

He nodded, and then, leaning down, he snatched up my camera bags from the floor. His eyes subtly assessed me as he rose, and I felt another surge of warmth. And want.

"Come." Again, Lucien beckoned for me to follow. "I think you'll find the lighting in the study will work best for this shoot."

Normally, I would insist on choosing the setting for the shoot. I always decided where the lighting was best, and that was determined only after a careful inspection of multiple potential shooting sites.

But, today, I had no argument in me. I only wanted one thing, to follow Lucien. So follow him, I did. Like a puppy, I trailed behind him, struggling to keep up with his long, sure strides.

We traveled down corridor after corridor. The house was enormous and like a huge, never-ending maze. I concluded rather quickly that I'd never find my way back to the front door, not without Lucien's help. Perhaps that was his goal? But instead of feeling uncomfortable and unsafe about that possibility, I felt nothing but calm and subdued.

In fact, I was kind of enjoying the feeling of being at Lucien's mercy.

With that thought passing through my head, we reached the study. The room did have fabulous lighting, I conceded as we walked in.

"Okay," I began, turning to face Lucien. "I should get set up so we can get started."

"Certainly," he replied.

I got set up, and ten minutes later, I was shooting what I knew would be some of the best photographs I'd ever taken. Lucien had been spot-on correct, the lighting was perfect. The blinds were drawn tightly on the outside world, but the many lamps scattered throughout the room cast my subject in just the right level of shades and shadows.

I took pictures of Lucien sitting pensively at his desk, pics of him standing at the windows with the blinds drawn, and a few final shots of him lounging on a red leather sofa against the far wall.

Lucien's casual attire and mussed hair provided the ideal contrast to what the piece was to be about— his power and wealth.

As I wrapped up, snapping one final shot of him standing directly in front of me, I said, "That was amazing, Lucien. I think the pictures are going to be phenomenal."

"I'm sure they will be stunning," he murmured, "with you behind the lens."

I thanked him, and said, "Well, you're a fantastic subject."

"I suppose we make a good team, then," he replied with a dazzling smile.

Oh, please, sweet baby Jesus, save my soul.

I hid behind the lens once more to conceal all the emotions Lucien was stirring in me.

A good team… I sighed.

"Let's take a few more shots," I said, just to give myself time to get my shit together.

Lucien was a few feet away when he looked up and asked in a low voice, "How do you want me, Dahlia?"

I gulped. "Uh, just like that."

I zoomed in on his face. "What color are your eyes?" I asked. "They're so…indecipherable."

He chuckled as he replied, "What color do you think they are, Dahlia?"

And in that moment, with time freezing for about three seconds, I saw the real Lucien Chambers.

"Dark brown?" I inquired shakily.

"Yes," he replied, "that's correct. My eyes are dark brown."

Still looking through the lens, poised to snap a single photo, I again saw a flash of the real Lucien Chambers. And, yes, his eyes were dark brown, but there was something more there, something deep, something beyond a mere shade or color. What was in Lucien's eyes was something indescribable.

It struck me then—his eyes betrayed that he was someone not entirely human.

Gasping, I stepped back, but not before I got in that one final shot.

"What are you?" I whispered as I lowered the camera to my side.

He came to me, his body inches from mine. "What do you mean?" he innocently inquired.

He was so male, so intoxicatingly male. His smell, the heat from his body... Suddenly, I didn't care if he was something other than human. In fact, that possibility made me more curious than ever. And my body responded accordingly. All I could think of was sex, sex with Lucien, sex with a man that was possibly something more than a man.

What would that be like?

Taking the camera from my grasp, Lucien smiled and asked, "May I take some photos of you, Dahlia?"

I was never one to have my picture taken, but with Lucien offering to go behind the lens, I didn't much care.

I nodded as I breathed out a sultry, "Yes."

"Great." He took a step back.

"What do you want me to do?" I inquired, glancing around the room.

Fidgeting with the camera settings, he distractedly gestured for me to go to the red leather couch. "Lie down on the sofa," he said. "I think your hair will look nice up against the leather."

"Auburn on crimson," I said, giggling.

I was feeling strange, kind of drunk. What was he doing to me?

"Yes," Lucien agreed, "there is that. The auburn on crimson, as you put it. But I'm also curious to see how your porcelain pale skin looks against the bright red."

I nodded, acquiescing. I was eager to please Lucien, so I went to and leaned back on the sofa, carefully so as to avoid placing the heels of my boots on the supple leather.

When the bottom hem of my wrap dress fell away, exposing the creamy skin of one thigh, I hurriedly adjusted the fabric.

"Oh," I said, "I'm sorry."

"Don't apologize." Lucien sauntered over to where I was awkwardly lying on the sofa. He helped me scoot up and positioned me the way he wanted— up against the plush leather arm. Gently, he drew my auburn hair off to one side and brought it around to the front.

I let out a nervous laugh, but the truth was I was feeling even more turned on than earlier, so much so that I didn't mind one bit when Lucien's fingers trailed down from my neck to my chest.

He lingered. His eyes met mine as he toyed with the silky, green material barely covering my cleavage. "May I," he asked. His fingers grazed my skin, creating a heated path.

"Yes," I replied, my chest heaving with excited breaths.

With his eyes still holding mine in a seeming trance, he opened the front of my dress, exposing both of my breasts. I leaned back my head and gasped as his knuckles grazed over my left nipple, the peak aching to be touched by him.

"There," he said softly, "let's start like that."

Scooting back, he took a couple of shots. "Look at me, Dahlia," he suddenly commanded.

I did as he asked.

Snap. Snap. Snap.

"Open your dress a little more."

I did as he asked.

Snap. Snap. Snap.

"Show me a little more thigh."

I did that, too.

Snap. Snap. Snap.

And then he was back in front of me, his hand at the ribbon sash keeping the dress from falling completely open.

"How would you feel if we were to lose the

dress?" he asked.

I stared into his eyes. *So mesmerizing.* I'd never felt as sexy as I did in that moment. I also never felt as turned on.

I licked my lips, and he asked with a smirk, "Does this, my photographing you, excite you?"

"Yes," I whispered.

"Do *I* turn you on, Miss Vaughn?"

"Call me Dahlia," I murmured. "Remember. We're on a first-name basis."

"Yes, Dahlia," he purred. "Now, answer the question."

"Yes," I admitted. A flood of heat hit me, making me moan and arch my back. "You turn me on."

I was so wet, so fucking dripping wet. I wanted him to touch me. I *needed* him to touch me. "Please," I begged.

"Please what?" he asked, like he had no clue.

But he knew. He was toying with me, but I didn't even give a damn.

Nimbly, I undid the tie on my dress. The fabric fell away, exposing all of me to Lucien. "Touch me," I pleaded.

And he did.

With the camera in one hand, he touched me with his other. He toyed with my breasts, caressed his knuckles down my abdomen, and placed two fingers at my core.

I gasped, "Ohh…"

He touched me gently, and I loved every minute of it. But when he slipped a finger into me, I jerked away.

"Are you untouched, Dahlia?" he asked, concern creasing his brow. *Or was that some other emotion?*

His finger remained in me, unmoving. And though it felt somewhat uncomfortable, I moved a little, instinct taking over.

"Dahlia?" he prompted, twisting his finger.

Wincing, I blurted, "Yes. I'm a virgin."

He smiled. "Oh, you just keep getting better and better."

I knew he'd handpicked me to photograph him, but had I been chosen for some other reason? Had this always been his intent—to touch me sexually?

It didn't matter, because in that moment, I knew this was the man I wanted to give my virginity to.

"You can do more," I told him.

His eyebrows went up. "How much more?" he wanted to know.

"As much as you want."

His eyes assessed me. "I *can* make it so it won't hurt," he offered, his tone soft.

"I think that's impossible," I laughed.

But there was no jest in his tone when he replied, "Anything is possible with me, Dahlia."

"Anything?"

"Yes, anything…and everything."

Before I could ask him what he meant, his mouth was on me, lapping at my folds and pulling my clit into his mouth with his teeth. One finger was still inside of me, but this time, when he moved, it no longer hurt. Not even when he drove in and out of me relentlessly. He added another finger, and then another. Even filled with half of Lucien's large hand, I felt no pain. The only thing I felt was pleasure and this wonderful build up.

But before I fell over the edge, Lucien's fingers left me, and he began kissing his way up my body. His hot mouth stopped and suckled at my breasts, and then he kissed up my neck until he covered my mouth with his. As his tongue danced with mine, I felt dizzy with lust, dizzy with him.

Giggling against his lips, I tugged at his sweater. "Off," I demanded.

Lucien leaned back and slipped the fine cashmere over his head, mussing his hair up further. His chest was smooth and a golden tan tone, I supposed thanks to his Spanish mother. He was handsome in a timeless way.

He undid his pants, but before he took them off, I placed my hand over his. "Wait," I said.

"Having second thoughts?"

"No." I shook my head. "I'm just feeling nervous, I guess."

"Look at me, Dahlia," he said softly.

Deep into his eyes I peered, until suddenly I was no longer nervous or frightened.

"How do you do that?" I asked.

But Lucien didn't provide me with any explanation. Instead, he urged me up so he could slide my gaping dress the rest of the way off.

"What about my boots?" I asked as the dress fell to the floor.

"Leave them," he said.

He then removed what remained of his clothing and knelt down on the floor in front of the sofa. I was still sitting up from when he'd taken off my dress, and he put his hand on my shoulder and urged me back.

My bare skin pressed into the supple leather. It all felt so hot and decadent, so I spread my legs and wrapped them around Lucien's narrow hips.

Smiling in a knowing way, he fitted himself to me... And then, he was inside of me, sheathed to the hilt.

Strangely, I felt not an ounce of pain. Lucien had apparently kept his word. There was nothing but pleasure. And when he moved, ecstasy overcame me.

I was no expert in sex, only knowing what I'd read and what Veronica had told me, but I knew this was different. Better. Lucien's cock was like an instrument, and he played it unbelievably well.

Drawing my hips up, he thrust in and out of me with abandon, and within minutes, I reached the apex.

I felt him swell within me. He grew even harder. He wanted more, and I wanted more.

Lucien withdrew and pulled me down to the floor with him. He turned me around, bent me over the sofa, and had me like that. I felt my knees graze on what I was sure was an authentic Persian rug, but there was no pain.

Lucien wrapped his hand in my hair as he continued to fuck me. He was untiring, but so was I. I wanted more; I'd become as insatiable as he. We fucked on the floor, and we fucked on his desk. He had me up against the wall, and in his huge desk chair. The boots came off at some point and he made me lick up the leather sides while I kneeled at his feet, boots dangling from his hand. I was commanded to lick him, and I obliged, savoring every inch of him before I took him fully in my mouth.

As the night wore on, time became lost. I discovered I wasn't me. I was a body made for sex. I was pulled, pushed, bit, tasted, and filled in every way, *every* way. Not even *that* hurt. I just looked into Lucien's eyes before he turned me around, and then all I felt as he pushed into another previously untouched place was indescribable pleasure.

When everything was over, I lay curled up on the floor. Lucien was nestled behind me. When my body came back down to Earth, I felt his touch everywhere. I tasted him in my mouth, my skin felt seared with him, and my body was filled with him. I was high on Lucien Chambers, and every part of me tingled in the aftermath of too many orgasms to count and too much of him.

"You're not an ordinary man, are you?" I mumbled weakly.

Lucien pulled me closer to him and kissed the top of my head. "No, Miss Vaughn, I am not an ordinary man."

Nestled in his arms, I felt so soothed and comforted. It was like I had come home. Still, I had many more questions. However, I was unable to articulate a single one.

Empty of myself, yet filled with the essence of Lucien, I fell asleep.

chapter
THREE

woke with my cheek pressed to new carpeting. As I inhaled the scent of fresh glue and fibers, I knew I was no longer at Lucien's house. I'd been returned to my apartment with the recently redone floors.

Rolling onto my back, I thought about the night before. The last memory I had was of Lucien confirming that he was no ordinary man. Then, I had dozed off.

"What is he?" I questioned as I stared up at the ceiling.

Suddenly, with those words uttered and out there, all my senses came back to me, and, dear God, I felt everything.

Letting out a litany of, "Ouch-ouch-ouch," I rolled

to my side and curled up in a fetal position.

Every part of me hurt like hell. The silky fabric of the green wrap dress, which had been placed back on me, rubbed at my sore nipples. My legs ached, and my rug-burned back and knees were on fire.

But the worst pain by far was between my legs.

Lucien Chambers had definitely *had* me in every way possible, and I was feeling all the sexual fury he'd unleashed on me in all my secret places. Even so, beyond the discomfort, I felt myself grow wet.

How could that be? I wondered.

But sure enough, the mere thought of Lucien and the things we'd done made me wild with lust. Aroused, I trailed my hands down my body and untied my dress. I wanted to be naked, and soon I was.

As I writhed wantonly on the carpeting, I wished Lucien were here to give me more of what I'd had last night. Reaching between my legs, I spread the growing dampness with my fingers. I touched myself gently, at first, but that was not enough. I rubbed more vigorously, almost to the point of passing-out painful, sensitive as I was. Memories of the prior night fueled my actions, though, and moaning for the man who'd unleashed this wild side of me, I brought myself to orgasm.

With a final shudder of release, I whispered his name, "Lucien."

I didn't know what he was or what he had done to me. But there was one thing I was sure of—I wanted more.

After a long, hot shower, I wrapped a thick chenille robe around my body. Relaxed, for now, I made a cup of coffee and decided to download the photographs I'd taken of Lucien to my computer. As I was attaching the cable from the camera to the computer at my desk, my cell phone rang.

Glancing down, I saw it was Veronica calling.

"Shit." I bumped my cup as I picked up the phone, and liquid spilled onto the desk surface. Quickly, I mopped up the mess with the sleeve of my robe.

When I finally placed the phone back to my ear, I could hear Veronica saying, "Dahlia, are you there? What's going on?"

"Hey, I'm here," I replied as I settled back in my seat. "I just spilled a little coffee. Everything is fine."

"Fine, really?" Veronica scoffed. "Where have you been? I called you a dozen times last night." She sighed. "Didn't you get any of my messages, Dahlia?

How'd it go with Lucien? Damn, did you even come home last night?"

I swiveled in the desk chair, pondering how much I should tell Veronica.

"Dahlia," Veronica said slowly, "are you there?"

"Yes, yes," I replied. "I'm here."

"What's wrong with you?" she asked, but before I had a chance to reply, she burst out with an exuberant, "Oh, my God, you *didn't* come home last night, did you?"

"Uh…"

"Holy shit, I can't believe it." Veronica sounded stunned. Excitedly stunned, but stunned nonetheless. "Did you lose your virginity to Lucien-fucking-Chambers?"

"Um…"

"You were with him, I know it," she declared. "I hear it in your voice, Dahl. Something is different with you."

Ha, understatement of the year. Something sure was different with me. I'd gone from a virginal, scared young woman to a lustful, horny-ass vixen. All thanks to Lucien and whatever crazy powers he had over me.

Clearing my throat, I admitted the truth to my cousin. Not all of it, of course, but I did tell her, "Yes,

Veronica, it's true. Lucien Chambers took my v-card."

"I knew it!" she exclaimed. "Damn, it must've been good, too. You sound more relaxed than I've ever heard you."

Was I ever! But I also had a concern, a concern for my heart. "I feel so strongly about him now, Veronica. Is this what love feels like?"

"Hardly," she scoffed. "But I'd say you're definitely in lust."

"Yeah..." I trailed off. I couldn't argue that one.

Veronica cleared her throat and whispered, "Did it hurt a lot? Are you feeling okay today? I hope he was gentle with you."

Not exactly, I thought. To my cousin, though, I said, "It didn't hurt at all last night. I felt great, but today" — I blew out a breath — "I'm feeling everything."

I winced at the reminder of my many sore spots.

"What do you mean it didn't hurt last night?" Veronica asked, confused. "My first time was agonizing."

"Umm..."

This was my chance to come clean. Maybe Veronica could help me figure out what Lucien was. But it felt so silly now to think he was anything more than a man. He was probably just a very skilled man, right?

Still, how could just peering into his eyes have made me feel so giddy, so drunk on lust? And how was he able to lessen the pain of losing my virginity? He had taken me so many times, in so many ways, but nothing he'd done to me had hurt. Well, at least, not at the time. Last night, everything was pure pleasure.

"Dahlia, are you still there?" Veronica prompted when I grew silent.

"I'm here, I'm here," I said, and after a pause, I asked, "Hey, can you do a favor for me?"

"Sure, honey," she replied.

"Can you do a little research on Lucien? I couldn't come up with much before the shoot, but you're much more of a pro at digging and finding out the good stuff."

"Of course," Veronica said. Then, after a beat, she added softly, "You like him now, don't you?"

It was true. I liked Lucien — a lot.

"Yeah, I kind of do like him," I quietly admitted.

I felt a new pain with my admission, a pain in my heart. Was Lucien doing this to me, too? Making me yearn for him?

But Veronica had an alternative explanation: "He's your first, Dahl. Those strong feelings are to be expected."

"I suppose," I murmured. Still, I knew what I was

feeling was something more.

Before we disconnected, I reminded Veronica, "Call me if you come up with something on Lucien. Anything at all, okay?"

I wanted the dirt, and my cousin was good at uncovering exactly that.

"Sure," she replied. "And don't worry, Dahlia. If he has any skeletons, I'll find them."

On that note, we ended the call.

Ten minutes later, I was still at the desk. My eyes were glued to the computer screen and the image that was on it.

"No fucking way," I murmured as I stared and stared. Disbelief at what I was seeing was my primary feeling.

Twenty minutes later, I'd still not moved.

Thirty minutes — the same.

All due to what was on the screen before me.

So what was so compelling?

There was one picture filling the screen, a picture from the night before, a picture of Lucien. It was the final photo I had taken of him, when he had stood before me with his dark eyes betraying that he was *something else.*

I'd already scanned through the photos he'd taken of me afterward, the many sexual shots on the red leather sofa. Those images had not bothered me one bit. Peering at them had made me think of Lucien and the things he'd done to me. Smiling, I had moved those photos to a folder marked "Private."

And then I'd come across this picture, the one I could not turn away from. All of the other photos of Lucien had turned out incredible. I had printed a bunch with the intention of choosing the best shots for the magazine spread. Then, at one point, I'd come across this single image of Lucien—a close-up of his face—and that is what now held me captive.

In the picture, Lucien appeared as perfect as always—dark and sultry eyes, great bone structure, full lips curved up in a knowing grin. But there was something different, something in his eyes. It was the same something I'd glimpsed briefly last night, that moment after I'd looked through the lens and asked him about the color of his eyes.

The moment I saw the real him.

And here it was, documented. What I'd seen was *real*. That glimpse of otherworldliness Lucien had allowed me to see hadn't been my imagination, after all. And now, like last night, in the image on the screen, Lucien Chambers' beautiful, deep brown eyes were again not quite human. There was something feral in his gaze, something inexplicable. There was no single word or way to accurately describe what the image portrayed, but you knew when you saw it that something was off. Off in a way that was beautiful and appealing, but off nonetheless.

"Did he want me to see this?" I asked out loud, my own voice causing me to jump.

Perhaps, I concluded. Last night, Lucien had had no qualms about letting me know he was "no ordinary man."

But to have given me proof — this photo — I couldn't wrap my head around his reasoning.

It led me to one question, a question that simultaneously thrilled and scared me — what the hell did Lucien Chambers want from me?

chapter FOUR

"Holy shit, Dahlia, wait until you hear what I found out about your friend Lucien."

Friend? I let out a light laugh. To me, he was so much more than that.

Veronica continued, breathless, ignoring my snicker. Damn, this had to be good. "I dug deep," she said. "And let's just say I discovered some really weird shit."

"Like what?" I ventured.

"You sure you want to hear what I found?"

I needed to know who—and what—Lucien was, so I plopped down on the sofa, cradled the phone to my ear, and said, "Yeah, I'm ready. Hit me with what you've got."

I listened as Veronica took a deep breath. Gearing up, I supposed, before she began with, "Well, there are rumors and undisclosed reports — and these were *not* easy to find, Dahl — that Lucien's mother practiced some kind of witchcraft in her younger years."

"What?" I dragged out the *a*, stupefied. "That is so bizarre, Veronica. Who are your sources exactly?"

"I can't say, hon, but there's more if you want to hear it."

"Okay." My voice had become soft and reticent, as had my attitude. I was afraid of what might come next. I was also worried that I'd gotten Veronica into something that could turn out to be dangerous. I mean, come on, this had to be some super-confidential information.

"Well," Veronica went on, "there are also rumors that Lucien's father is some kind of black magic expert."

I rolled my eyes. "Oh, please. Is there even such a thing? I thought all that black magic crap was made-up stuff for books and movies. What could really exist for someone to be an 'expert' in?"

"I don't know," Veronica replied. "Maybe that's how he met Lucien's mother. You know, if the rumors about her and the witchcraft are to be believed."

"That's just it," I said. "Who would believe such

a thing?"

I tried to make my tone light and dismissive, but the truth was I could see how those rumors might be true. Witchcraft, black magic, it would certainly explain Lucien's incredible success in every endeavor, his parents' success, too. And it provided an explanation for the something-other-than-a-man look in Lucien's eyes, both in person and in that damn photo.

"Hey, I don't know what's true and what's not," Veronica continued. "I'm just reporting the facts to you as I found them."

"I know, I know." I sighed. "And I appreciate all your work, V, I do. It's all just so unbelievable."

I had to keep up my farce of disbelief. I didn't want my cousin involved more than she already was.

But when Veronica quietly muttered, "Maybe Lucien is, like, some kind of magical being or something," she unknowingly took the words that'd been floating around in my head and made them seem more plausible.

"Oh, I don't know," I said, backtracking to throw her off. "This all sounds kind of silly."

Silly, but accurate, I secretly thought.

Veronica was silent for a long period, and then she said, "Well, silly or not, Dahlia, please promise me you'll stay away from Lucien Chambers."

That was a promise I could not make.

My restlessness extended throughout the remainder of the day. I was useless. I didn't even bother getting dressed. Instead, I lazed around in my robe, trying to read, trying to watch TV. But my mind was in one place and one place only—on Lucien.

I printed out the picture of Lucien—the one of him with the inhuman eyes—and carried it to the bedroom with me.

"What are you?" I asked the image as I sprawled back on the bed and held the photo high above my head.

Perhaps Lucien *was* some kind of a magical being. Or maybe he practiced magic of some sort and this was how he looked at those times. He'd certainly done something to me last night. I'd been under his spell, no doubt.

As I stared up at the photo, I half-expected the image to come alive. But, of course, that didn't happen. What did occur, though, were more feelings of arousal and more wanton need.

I undid the sash on the robe and touched myself again and again. I was unstoppable. I brought myself to orgasm so many times I lost count. By nightfall, I was spent and drenched in sweat. One thing for sure, I needed a shower.

Nude, I got up and walked to the bathroom. After lazily turning on the water, I stepped into the shower stall. I still felt kind of out of it, but the hot water calmed me. I stood for what felt like an eternity, until I finally picked up the loofah and soap and washed away everything.

I tried to think of nothing, but thoughts of Lucien broke through my weak mental defenses. I wondered if I'd hear from him again. Would he realize he'd allowed his *real* self to be seen in that one picture? If that was the real him — and I felt certain it was — then perhaps he'd feel compelled to stop me from turning it in for publication.

Would I do that? Turn the photo in and reveal him to the world?

No, never. I would protect what he had shared with me.

But he didn't need to know that.

Suddenly, I felt like I had a way to ensure Lucien would see me again. And it was time to capitalize on it.

It was juvenile and unprofessional, yes, but after wrapping myself up in a large white towel, I headed back out to the living room to find my cell so I could call Lucien.

"Mr. Chambers," I began hesitantly when he answered on the second ring.

My heart raced, I was so nervous. This was his private line, and I was not supposed to even have the number. But I'd jotted the digits down when I first received the particulars of the shoot. Someone had left the number printed in the margins on a sheet of information.

Lucien had to be surprised to hear from me, and I assumed his initial silence was an indicator that that was the case.

At last, he cleared his throat. "Miss Vaughn," he said, "may I ask where you obtained this number? It is a private line, after all."

"Uh…"

I was stumbling, and Lucien spoke right over me, his tone becoming terser and terser. "This number is for friends. It's for people I *choose* to talk to. I don't recall giving it to you. So I must inquire, is there a reason why you're contacting me —"

"You, you…" I stammered, interrupting. Now, I was mad. What a prick.

" —on my private line," he continued as if I'd never spoken.

I passed mad and landed at fuming. What an arrogant, pompous ass. And to think I'd spent the whole day thinking of him, feeling aroused by him, touching myself while looking at images of him. For the love of God, I'd given him my virginity. *Asshole.*

"First off," I began, "you have some nerve acting as if we're strangers."

"Sorry to break it to you," Lucien stated matter-of-factly, "but we *are* strangers."

It was all I could do to keep from climbing through the phone and throttling him. If I could have, I would have.

"I'd hardly call us strangers after the things that occurred last night," I volleyed back.

He barked out a laugh. "One night of sex doesn't make us friends all of the sudden."

"It makes us something," I retorted.

What was I even going on about? I knew I had no real right to make any demands. He was essentially correct, but still, he had me so pissed.

And then he had the guile to laugh, like a deep, fully amused chuckle.

"Well, I'm glad you find this so amusing, Mr. Chambers," I said in the coolest of tone. "I'm sure the general public will find it infinitely amusing, as well, when they see the, let's say, very interesting shot I took of you." *Take that*, I silently added.

I braced myself for his wrath…but nothing happened.

The jerk had hung up on me.

chapter FIVE

expected Lucien to show up on my doorstep in a fury. I expected him to demand for me to give him the incriminating picture...or else. I, at the very least, expected him to call back and try to work something out with me. I mean, what if I was serious about my threat? What if I exposed him?

But none of what I expected to occur happened.

I heard not a single word from the mysterious man...if he even was a man.

One day turned to two then two days turned to three.

It was that awkward time of the year, between Christmas and New Year's, where nobody seemed to be working. Everyone was in a festive limbo, including me. Well, minus the festive. I was actually in more of a down limbo.

The day before New Year's Eve, I got myself together and drove to the local mall. I had a few gifts to return and figured I might as well get out of the house and do something productive. I'd not left my apartment since speaking with Lucien, and, needless to say, it felt weird to be around so many people when I stepped in the mall.

I hadn't minded the solitude at my apartment. I had spent the time alone watching old Christmas movies and drinking too much coffee. Fueled on caffeine, I had done loads of laundry, cleaned out my closets, dusted, and vacuumed the new carpeting.

The goal, however, had been to not think of Lucien. And I'd been successful, for the most part. But here at the busy mall with the decorated trees and hanging garlands, the holiday tunes and the smell of cinnamon, I was reminded of Lucent Magazine's Christmas party, where I'd first laid eyes on Lucien Chambers in the flesh.

Sighing, I sat down on a bench outside of a store selling cookware. I needed a distraction, so I called Veronica. After all my alone time, I decided it was time to rejoin the land of the living.

After Veronica answered and we dispensed with

our greetings, I asked, "What are you doing tomorrow night?"

"It's New Year's Eve, silly. What do you think I'm doing?"

"Going out?"

"Yes, of course." Veronica sounded flabbergasted with my obtuseness. "Dahlia, don't you remember me inviting you to Solstice? There's a private party being held there to usher in the New Year in style."

Solstice was a high-end nightclub. They were hosting an upscale New Year's Eve private party this year. When I thought on it further, I did vaguely recall Veronica mentioning something about the party weeks ago. I had told her *no way* when she'd requested I join her.

"Oh, yeah," I murmured, "I remember now."

"Have you changed your mind about going?" she asked. Veronica sounded so hopeful that I silenced the "no" that was on the tip of my tongue.

What other options did I have, anyway? Lounging on the sofa all night, watching more TV? Or, God forbid, continuing to pine away for Lucien?

"Hell no," I mumbled.

Veronica replied with a confused, "Huh? Hell no to what?"

"Nothing, nothing." I swished my hand in the air

dismissively, and then I made what I hoped would be a good decision. "I think I'll tag along with you to the party. If that's okay, that is."

"Are you kidding?" I could hear the smile in Veronica's voice. "Of course it's okay. It's better than okay, in fact." She paused, and, clearly pleased with my change of heart, added, "I'm happy you're coming with, Dahl."

The next night found me rummaging through my closet. Sadly, I couldn't find a single thing to wear. I was going for sexy, but I was at a loss beyond the lingerie I'd picked out.

Sitting down on the edge of my bed in a black demi-bra, black panties, and black garters and stockings, I put my head in my hands, and lamented, "Ugh, I have nothing hot to wear to that damn party."

But then I recalled a dress I had bought in the fall. It was for another party, an art gallery opening I'd been invited to in September. I'd fallen ill and had not been able to attend. That dress would be perfect!

Jumping up, I returned to the closet and pushed the clothes and hangers aside as I dug to the back. "There it is," I said, sighing when I spotted black sequins sparkling in the dim closet lighting.

The dress was ideal for a New Year's Eve party, particularly one being held in such a high-end, trendy nightclub.

Pulling the hot little number off the hanger, I slipped it over my head and stood in front of a mirror. *Hmm...* The hemline was short, very short, and there was a plunging neckline where the sequined fabric draped down almost to my waist.

There's no way I can wear a bra with this dress, I determined.

After taking off the dress, I discarded the demi-bra I had put on earlier. Staring at my reflection in just panties, a garter belt, and stockings, I decided to lose the underwear, as well. Without the matching bra, the black panties just looked kind of off.

I felt like a slut, wearing nothing but a garter and stockings under such a revealing dress, but I kind of liked the feeling. I wished Lucien were here, as I wouldn't have minded being his slut for the night.

My breasts felt full and heavy, swelling at the mere thought of Lucien. My pink nipples pebbled and I brushed my fingers over them in response. The black garter belt accentuated my hips and contrasted with my creamy skin, particularly at the juncture between my thighs.

Quickly, I made myself think of something else. I was wasting no more time getting myself off every time I thought of Lucien. After hanging up on me, he didn't deserve that kind of attention.

For the second time, I slipped the dress back over my head. The tops of the stockings and clasps to the garter belt were left slightly exposed by the short length, but it all looked just right. With the plunging front showing off *all* of my ample cleavage, I felt ultra-sexy.

"Take that, Lucien," I said as I slipped on five-inch pumps and spun around once in front of the mirror.

At that exact moment, I knew what my New Year's resolution needed to be—no more thinking about Lucien Chambers. Not in any way, shape, or form.

chapter
SIX

usic pulsed all around in the club. It was dark, the industrial interior dimly lit. Every so often, strobe lights flashed rapidly, making everyone on the dance floor appear as if they were moving in slow motion.

"It's weird in here," I yelled to Veronica over the loud house music.

The name of the club, Solstice, was a reference to the winter solstice, and the club was thusly decorated as a winter wonderland. Everything was covered in faux ice and snow. I found it all quite realistic. So realistic, in fact, that I began to shiver in my skimpy dress, the sequins shimmering in the low lights.

Veronica leveled me with an are-you-serious

expression.

"What?" I asked.

"You," she said, pointing to me, "have *no* room to talk."

"What are you talking about?" I inquired. I truly had no idea what she meant.

But it all became clear when she replied, "Dahlia, you can't call a place weird when you yourself can't stay away from weird." She gestured to a crowd of men in suits, up on the second-floor level of the club.

My eyes followed her hand, and I uttered a quiet, "Oh," when I spotted one man in particular. That was who Veronica was referring to as *weird*.

The man emerged from the crowd of men, who were laughing, drinking, and talking. Casually, he leaned on the edge of the railing and peered down at me.

"Lucien," I whispered. "What is he doing here?"

Veronica rolled her eyes. "Please, Dahlia. You can't fool me. I know you must've invited him." Her gaze softened. "If you did, though, it's okay."

I swore to Veronica, "I didn't invite him, V."

"Well, he wasn't on the guest list."

When I glanced back up at the second floor, Lucien stepped out of sight. Sighing, I said, "Not being on the guest list wouldn't have mattered."

Veronica made a face, before taking a sip of her mixed drink. When she lowered her glass, she said, "Yeah, you're probably right."

Whatever the circumstances, I couldn't believe Lucien was here at the club. I just knew he was here because of me. But really, the nerve of that man! After his rebuff and dismissal when I dared to call his precious private line, you would think he'd be playing it cool and backing up his dismissive words by ignoring me. That would drive his point home, right?

But not only was Lucien not ignoring me, he was now making his way down to the first floor.

"Shit," I moved to hide behind a thick column of faux ice. "He's coming this way, V. We have to lose him."

Veronica peered in his direction. "Too late," she said, sighing. "He can see you hiding, you crazy bitch." She grabbed my arm and pulled me out from behind my icy cover. "You may as well give up on playing it cool."

"Yeah, I guess you're right," I murmured.

Veronica's eyes met mine. "Seriously, though, do you want me to get rid of him for you?"

I replied with an uncertain, "Yes?"

"Be cool, then." Veronica squared her shoulders

and encouraged me to do the same. "Just say hi, and then we'll send him on his way."

Like that was an easy task. It was laughable to think either of us could send Lucien Chambers on his way. I had the sense no one told him what to do... ever.

When Lucien reached us, he gave Veronica a curt nod and promptly zoned in on me.

"Miss Vaughn," he said, "I wanted to stop down and personally wish you a very happy New Year."

"Well, that's nice of you." I glanced at the time illuminated on my cell that was on the table. "But it's not quite midnight yet."

"No, it's not." His dark eyes seared into me, branding me. "However, if you'd be so inclined — and since it is *close* to midnight — I'd like to celebrate the ringing in of the New Year with you."

He offered me his hand, and I took it without hesitation. His skin was so warm, so inviting. I flushed with excitement.

Wow. It was like we'd never even had that heated conversation the other day. It was like Lucien hadn't heard me when I'd threatened him over the phone with the incriminating photograph. Or perhaps he didn't care. Like how I no longer cared that he'd dismissed me so coldly. I was supposed to be mad at him, yes, but who could stay angry when gazing into such mesmerizing eyes?

Not me, apparently.

Veronica cleared her throat, and I glanced over at her.

She frowned, and I shrugged.

Curtly, she said to Lucien, "Would it be okay if my cousin and I had a minute alone?"

Lucien let go of my hand and stepped away. "Certainly." He cleared his throat. "I need to freshen my drink, anyway." He lifted his empty rocks glass, a lock of dark hair falling to his forehead. He looked rakishly handsome before he spun around and walked away.

"Hot," I muttered to myself.

Veronica leaned into me and hissed, "Are you crazy? I thought you were planning on staying away from him."

"I never said that," I replied, in defense of my behavior.

"What? Five minutes ago, you wanted me to get rid of him, right?"

"Um…"

I thought I was done with Lucien too, after his terse treatment of me. But did I really want to stay away? "No," I replied.

"No what?" Veronica questioned.

"No," I stated more resolutely. "I don't want to stay away from him, and I don't want you, or anyone, to get rid of him for me."

She shook her head. "What is *wrong* with you, Dahlia?"

"I don't know," I whispered. It was the truth.

"You're acting so hot and cold."

Veronica sounded frustrated, and I couldn't blame her.

"I'm sorry," I whispered, eyes downcast.

I didn't understand my behavior, either. Lucien had this hold over me, particularly in person. That was the only explanation I could come up with.

Veronica shot a furtive glance to where Lucien was making his way back to us, fresh drink in hand. In a hushed voice, she said, "Look, I understand you're confused about your feelings for him. That's to be expected under the circumstances." She waved her hand around. "Losing your virginity to him and all. But I'm worried for you, Dahl. Sure, Lucien is gorgeous, rich, and successful, but there's something *off* about him."

"Appealingly *off*," I retorted.

"Dangerously *off*," she countered.

Lucien was well out of earshot, but I swear I

detected a hint of a smile on his face. He was well-aware that there was something *off* about him. And that was what made him so damn fascinating.

Turning to Veronica, I said, "Look, V, I'll be fine. I'm just going to talk to him for a little while, okay?"

She appeared skeptical. "Are you sure?"

"Yes." I motioned to her friends in the bar area. "Go hang with your friends. I'll re-join you guys later tonight."

"Okay," she said, relenting. "But for the record, know that I support you, Dahlia, but also know I really don't like this."

And with that, she walked away, giving Lucien a wide berth as she passed him.

He lowered his head and chuckled to himself. And then he came to me.

"Come, Dahlia," he beckoned.

"Where are we going?" I inquired.

"Somewhere more private."

My heart raced and my body immediately heated with desire. I was terrified, but so incredibly sexually excited. This man was going to be the death of me, I was sure of it.

But even that unsettling thought didn't stop me from smiling and saying, "Let's go."

chapter
SEVEN

aybe this man *was* capable of magic. Maybe he himself was filled with some kind of magical powers.

I wasn't sure, and it all seemed kind of nutty, but I had no other explanation for how I was able to so willingly forget his dismissive treatment of me on the phone.

But forget it I did.

I allowed Lucien to lead me away from the throngs of people. I allowed him to guide me—my hand in his—to a private, closed-off part of the club where the music was nothing but a distant echo of bass beats.

"This is a much more private spot for us to talk," he murmured as he led me farther and farther away from any lingering people.

Talk… Somehow I had a feeling we'd not be doing much *talking*.

We walked up three winding sets of metal rungs, my high heels making little *ting-tings* along the way.

"Am I walking too quickly for you?" Lucien asked, concerned, it seemed, as he slowed to a stop.

When he turned to me, one step higher than where I stood, I glanced up at him.

Beautiful, I thought as I gazed into his deep brown eyes. Everything looked normal, at first, but then I saw beyond Lucien's chiseled features, beyond his perfection. I saw myself reflected back to me in his gaze. And I knew then what he saw in me. I was what he ultimately wanted — innocence he'd corrupted.

As if on cue, the peaks of my breasts grew taut beneath the draped sequin material of my dress. "Are you doing this to me?" I inquired.

"No. Your reactions are your own."

"And you approve."

He nodded slowly, a smile curving one side of his mouth. "Yes, I approve."

The skin exposed at the tops of my stockings, and below the hem of my dress, suddenly felt all tingly. I somehow knew that in Lucien's eyes it looked creamy and inviting.

"Good enough to eat," he whispered.

And it was then I felt too exposed. Damn, my dress was entirely too short. Why had I worn it?

But these were not my thoughts, these were thoughts Lucien was putting in my head to mess with me.

"Stop it," I snapped.

"No," he retorted.

His control was unwavering. His will was ironclad, and I was no match. Again, Lucien asked why I'd worn the dress. He asked his question from inside *my* head.

"I wore it for you," I whispered, capitulating. "Part of me hoped you'd show up tonight. But you probably knew that already, right?"

No answer.

We were near the top of the steps, mere feet from the entrance to the private area to which he'd guided me. I thought we'd continue the rest of the way at this point, but we stayed where we were — Lucien one step above me.

Slowly, he reached out and moved aside the draped material at my chest, exposing one breast.

"I like this dress," he said. "And I'm glad you wore it."

He pinched one nipple, and I gasped from the

sharp pain. I was also instantly aroused. This state of arousal, however, was unlike all the other times I'd thought of Lucien, all the times I'd touched myself thinking of him. Almost unbelievingly, this was much more intense.

Lucien smiled, and I thought: *He must know my thoughts. If he can inject himself in my head, perhaps he can see what is in there, as well?*

"Not everything," he replied in a low, husky voice.

"You heard me in your head?"

"Yes."

"What are you?" I asked, peering up at him curiously.

I received no answer. Instead, he said, "I want that picture, Dahlia."

I shook my head. "No."

It was my only hold over him, my only power play.

"We'll see about that," he replied, smirking.

Lucien suddenly swept me up in his arms. His strength was amazing. He held me pressed to him with ease as he leaned down and kissed me ferociously. There were no other words to accurately describe his hunger, his desperate touches, or his exertion of power over me.

Finally, he lowered me so I could stand beside him on the step. I found my footing and waited while he moved one step lower, to the step I'd been standing on before he lifted me to him.

From this new vantage point, he crouched down, like a feral being, and ran a firm hand up my stocking-covered leg. Stopping at the garter, he rasped, "Sexy. You are so sexy."

"Lucien," I moaned.

His touch was already driving me wild with lust. I felt my pussy grow wetter and wetter. Lucien's strong hand trailed higher, and when he found me lacking panties—and dripping for him—he let out a lust-filled growl.

Kneeling on the step below me, he urged me to spread my legs wider. "Lean back and hold onto the railing," he ordered.

I did as commanded, and then Lucien lifted my dress and placed his head between my legs. He went at me like my folds were the most delicious treat, lapping and licking and doing things with his tongue that were decadent and sinful.

I gripped his dark hair, and gasped. "Yes, right there," when he drove his tongue up into me.

Pressing at just the right spot resulted in me coming...and coming...and coming. Finally spent, I almost crumpled to the ground. But Lucien kept me upright.

I thought it would all end there, I thought he would send me on my way. And I especially thought he would once again demand I relinquish the photograph of him, the incriminating shot that exposed him as something more than a mere man.

But none of those things happened.

Instead, Lucien gathered me in his arms and carried me the rest of the way up the stairs. He was surprisingly gentle, and I felt as if I were in some twisted fairytale where he was my prince. A dark prince, yes, but a prince nonetheless.

With his shoulder, he pushed open the glass door at the top and stepped into the private club. I glanced around. It seemed this was an area that had not been used in some time, as heavy cloths lay draped over furnishings that mostly consisted of high-backed chairs, low tables, and a single long sofa.

Lucien walked over to the sofa and deposited me on the covered cushions. "Take off your dress," he demanded as he kicked off his polished shoes.

I did as he requested, my dress coming off at the same instant he removed his suit jacket.

"Lay back," he commanded.

"Okay," I murmured.

I allowed my body to relax back into the plushy sofa. Surprisingly, the heavy cloth covering the piece of furniture was smooth, soft, and luxurious-feeling. I molded my almost-nude body into the cushions and giggled. As with the other times with Lucien, I felt like I was high. I suspected I was in some way—I was high on him. He had exerted his magic, or whatever, and I was drunk on him.

What weird powers he possessed.

I felt so giddy, so aroused. It was the strangest combination. I writhed on the sofa, allowing the soft covering to bunch up between my legs. Giggling, I collapsed to my stomach, and when my breasts rubbed against more luxurious material, I moaned.

With the fabric still bunched between my legs, Lucien wound his fingers in the softness and began to move the luxurious material back and forth against my throbbing clit. "Do you like that?" he asked.

I groaned out, "Yes," and he continued, bringing me to a quick orgasm. I arched up as I came. I was naked, except for the stockings and garter, and Lucien's eyes zoned in on the lingerie.

His gaze was hungry, and I seductively asked, "Should I take these off?"

I snapped the garter, the sting feeling good against my hypersensitive skin.

Lucien loosened his tie, his eyes never leaving me. "No," he replied.

I was on my knees, and when I began to lower my hips to the sofa Lucien stopped me. "No. Keep that ass up," he commanded.

"All right," I said, complying.

Lucien unzipped his pants and positioned himself behind my kneeling and arched-for-him form. I kind of liked the imbalance in power—me helpless and basically naked, and him clothed and in control.

He grasped my hair and urged my face down into the cushions, his hard cock nudging at my slick core. "Do you want this?" he asked, pushing in only a fraction of his substantial length.

"Yes," I replied, my voice muffled.

No sooner had the word left my mouth and Lucien was thrusting into me, pounding and pounding. This was so much harder than the other time we'd been together. But I loved it. And like the first time, I felt only pleasure.

But at some point, Lucien let up on whatever magic he was sending my way, and the pain of his primal, relentless thrusts became unbearable. Sensitive parts of me that had not healed from the first go-round with him throbbed. Scooting forward, I held onto the arm of the sofa and pulled away. But Lucien was right there on me.

Crying out, I tried again to get away. "Wait," I pleaded.

He wrapped his hand in my auburn tresses and wrenched my head back. His cock was inside me to the hilt as he asked, "Is this too much?"

"Maybe," I said, my breaths labored. "I think I might need a rest."

Lucien chuckled. "Too bad, Miss Vaughn. There is no rest for the wicked." His tone was unapologetic as he drove into me harder than ever, and added, "And you, my dear, are very wicked. Teasing me, taunting me. You're going to take everything I give you tonight."

He was so rigid, so swollen, and there was no escaping him. I should never have taunted him with the photo. With every frenzied thrust, I feared he might break me in two.

But then a strange thing happened.

I felt myself molding to him, *savoring* him. I let go, giving myself over to Lucien. And in that moment of succumbing, there was suddenly no more pain.

"See," he murmured as he leaned over me and whispered in my ear, "it's so much better, much easier for you, when you don't fight me."

"Yes," I agreed.

And it was easier, better. Giving in to Lucien was the key. So I let go. I gave him my body, and I gave him my mind.

And he took all I gave.

Soon, I felt Lucien *everywhere* inside of me.

He banded his arms around me. He played with my breasts with one hand, while his other hand caressed my clit. And all the while, the hard fucking continued. Continued and continued, well into the night and straight into the morning. It was hours and hours of unparalleled ecstasy. There was no more discomfort, only wave after wave of mind-blowing pleasure.

But then it all came to an end.

Before Lucien left me, lying on the covered sofa, naked and exhausted, he whispered in my ear, "Happy New Year, Dahlia."

"Happy New Year, Lucien," I rasped, my voice but a ragged whisper.

He laughed.

And then he left.

But I knew I'd see him again, seeing as I still had the picture he wanted.

chapter
EIGHT

"What the hell, Dahlia? What in God's name happened to you last night? I was searching all over, but I gave up, assuming you left."

I woke to Veronica's voice and her hands on me. She was trying to cover my bare body with a sheet. I was so sore, my muscles aching, my skin tender to the touch.

"No," I mumbled as I pushed her — and the sheet — away.

"Come on," she said, her tone coaxing. "Sit up a bit. Work with me here."

I opened my eyes, but things were blurry. I was hung-over from my time with Lucien. He had ravaged me all night, and I knew I probably looked a wreck as a result. Veronica appeared exhausted, as well. Her make-up was smeared, and there were dark circles under her eyes. Still, I could only imagine how much worse I looked.

Reluctantly, I sat up and allowed her to wrap the sheet around my shoulders. My dress was on the floor, and she picked it up. "I suppose you and Lucien worked things out?"

Her tone, though light, was laced with disapproval. She raised an eyebrow when I neglected to respond, and I shrugged my shoulders. "Uh, I guess. We didn't really talk all that much, though."

Veronica sighed. "Dahlia…" She shook her head. "Let's get you dressed and back to your apartment, okay?"

I nodded. "Okay."

Though she said nothing more, I saw in Veronica's eyes what she was thinking. My cousin thought me a fool. I'd allowed Lucien to do with me whatever he wanted, and I was again left with no answers.

Only more questions.

One thing I was certain of was that Lucien would find a way to see me again. Had he arranged to attend the

New Year's party once he found out—however that was—that I would be there? I highly suspected so.

"He'll see me again," I told my reflection the evening of the first day of the New Year.

I was back at my apartment, courtesy of Veronica. She'd helped me get into my dress back at the club, and then driven me home. We'd been so exhausted that we hadn't discussed much beyond how we couldn't wait to get some sleep.

I'd lain down immediately upon entering my bedroom, and then I'd slept for hours, dead to the world.

It was now nine in the evening. I'd eaten, but I still needed to take a shower. I was covered in dried sweat and God knew whatever else from my time with Lucien and the things we'd done.

Brushing my hair in front of the mirror above my dresser, I scanned my naked body.

There were light bruises and marks all over me from my night with Lucien. Nothing I couldn't handle, though. Even the soreness I'd felt for so many days seemed to be dissipating, which was odd. My discomfort should have been worse today, certainly not better.

"It's because you're becoming his," I whispered to my reflection. "You're giving in to him."

"Yes, you are," a deep voice rang out from behind me, startling me so much that I jumped and spun around.

Shit, Lucien Chambers was in my bedroom.

"H-how did you get in here?" I stuttered in a shaky voice.

I was frightened, but I was also thrilled to see Lucien again so soon.

chapter NINE

"Does it matter how I got in?" he asked, striding toward me. "The more apt question is: do you want me to leave?"

"Yes," I replied, covering my naked body with my hands. "I mean no."

He reached where I stood. I expected him to touch me, but he didn't.

Peering down at me, Lucien—so tall and foreboding, me so weak and small—asked, "Well, which one is it, Miss Vaughn? Yes…or no?"

"Dahlia," I whispered. "Call me by my first name."

I was tired of formalities. We'd broken through all that crap our first night together. Or so I had thought. But the walls had been re-erected when I'd called him and he had so unkindly reminded me that we were essentially strangers. But surely all the things we'd done last night called for an intimacy beyond last names.

Lucien saw this in my eyes and read this in my head. He knew, and he said to me accordingly, "As you wish, Dahlia."

I reached for a robe, but his strong hand caught my outstretched arm. "No," he said curtly. "Stay as you are. You want honesty? Then keep yourself uncovered."

Somehow I knew he meant more than my naked body. "You want my mind, as well?"

"I want all of you, Dahlia."

"So, take all of me," I urged.

And he did.

Lucien came at me. He picked me up and tossed me on the bed like I was a rag doll. "Oh," I breathed out, excited by an even more aggressive version of him.

"Look at me," he said, garnering my attention.

I watched as he took off all of his clothes, exposing his lean and sculpted body to my hungry gaze.

I wanted him so much.

Spreading my legs so he could see the effect he had on my body, I asked, "Do you do this to me?"

He stepped closer to the bed and dipped a finger between my legs. "As I told you last night, Dahlia, your reactions to me are your own."

I fell onto my back and let him finger me. I spread my legs farther in an invitation for him to do with my body whatever he desired. But Lucien slid his fingers out of me.

"Why are you stopping?" I asked.

"I'm not," he said as he crawled up the bed. "I'm just getting started." He hovered over me, lowering his hips to the juncture between my thighs.

With his throbbing cock pressing at my entrance, he asked, "Do *you* do this to *me*?"

"You tell me," I said.

With that, he thrust into me—encompassing me, owning me. I thought things would become rough and harsh, as they had the night before, but Lucien stilled and peered down at me. In a pained voice, he admitted, "You are my weakness, Dahlia."

His eyes were normal tonight, no otherworldliness. I stared up into the rich brown pools, searching for more. I wanted to find meaning behind his words, more insight into this man...if he even was just a man. I also longed to ask how *I* could be *his* weakness, when it seemed the exact opposite was true.

But there was no chance to discern or ask anything.

Lucien buried his face in the crux of my neck, and then got down to the business of fucking me senseless.

Time ceased to exist. The pleasure I experienced with him was again unparalleled. My entire body — no, my entire being — became one with Lucien. There was no more him and me, there was only us.

Afterward, I slept encircled in his strong arms. But unfortunately, when I awoke, he was gone from my bed.

"Lucien," I called out.

Silence.

I sat up and pulled the sheet we'd left wrinkled and damp around my bare body. It was then I noticed all my bruises and marks from our earlier encounters were gone.

"That's impossible," I murmured.

But no, the truth was before me. I was healed.

Lucien had healed me. Now, I really needed to see him.

I knotted the sheet at my chest to keep it in place and stood. I hurried to the living room, but no one was there.

Lucien Chambers was gone. I felt it in my heart.

Collapsing onto the sofa, I let out a long breath. "No," I cried out. "He can't be gone."

I shifted my weight and felt something slide

beneath me. Lifting my ass, I glanced down to see what was there.

Aah, all the photographs I'd printed.

Quickly, I moved aside and gathered the images. All the shots of Lucien appeared to be in order.

But wait… All were accounted for, except for one.

"No, no, no," I cried as I dropped the photos back onto the sofa and raced over to the computer.

It seemed to take forever to boot up. "Come on, come on," I urged the machine.

At last, when everything was up and running I accessed my folders. The folder marked *Private* — the one with all the sexy shots of me — was still there, as was the folder with the normal pics of Lucien. I opened that folder, and like with all the printed pictures, the pictures I'd taken of him were in order.

Except for one…one picture had been deleted.

"You erased it," I whispered. "And you took the one printed photo that could have exposed you for who you really are. You took the one picture that would show the world you're more than just a man."

In my head I heard Lucien laughing. Laughing, as he admitted, "Yes, Dahlia, I took the photo. I took what you should never have captured."

And in that instant, all went silent.

There was no more Lucien in my head, and my

body no longer felt in that constant state of arousal.

I felt only two things now — tired and spent.

I would never again see Lucien. Sure, I might run into him somewhere someday, but our time together as I knew it, however short, was over.

Bereft in a profound way, I crumpled to the ground.

I would complete my assignment, I vowed. I'd turn in the shots of Lucien. They were good photographs, capturing a confident and successful business man, but I no longer cared about the accolades I'd receive.

I felt too lost to care about anything.

How could I ever forget what I knew about Lucien Chambers? I had seen more, been touched by more. I was different now because of the things he'd exposed to me. I knew in my soul I was still connected to Lucien in some visceral way. He may have tried to break our connection, but it was still there. Faintly, yes, but not completely severed.

So where was I supposed to go from here?

EPILOGUE

*D*ays passed, weeks passed, months passed. My photos of Lucien ran in the magazine. I received several accolades, as I'd expected. I even won a small award.

But it all meant nothing.

I got up every day. I ate, I showered, I worked, and I slept. On the weekends, I spent time with Veronica, watching movies or ordering in food. I never went out socially. I had no desire to date or meet men.

How could any man ever compare to what I had experienced?

Veronica tried to cheer me up, but it was of no use. I was empty, incomplete. Something was missing. And I knew what that something was—Lucien.

It was ridiculous of me to hold onto him like this.

He'd moved on. There were photos of him out with models — dating, living his life. Never a clear shot of him, he didn't allow that, but the paparazzi had caught him out a time or two.

On a wintry March morning, with a thick carpet of snow still on the ground, I bundled up in a heavy sweater, high boots, and a bulky coat, and drove north of the city.

"This is crazy," I told myself as I pulled into a lot in a public park, a public park not far from Lucien's estate. The park was empty, save for a flock of Canada geese out on the ice-covered lake.

"I need to do this," I whispered, glancing up at my reflection in the rearview mirror.

I looked tired, with dark circles under my eyes. The past two months had been rough. No Lucien, no hits of whatever it was he gave to me.

Well, I was here to get my fix, even if it was only from afar.

I got out of the car and walked in the direction of Lucien's estate, trudging through heavy drifts of snow like they were nothing. I was on a mission.

I'd not felt Lucien's presence in so long. This was my experiment to see if narrowing the geography between us would result in re-establishing his connection with me. I'd not felt him in my head since the morning he'd left me.

We were still tethered, though, and I missed him.

Continuing on through the heavy snow, I worked my way to the edge of the lake. With no leaves on the trees, I was hoping Lucien's mansion would be visible up at the northernmost tip of the large body of water.

So, I headed north.

Unfortunately, it was slow going as there was lots of ice around the lake. I walked and walked, still, and as I made my way along the lake shore, the geese honked at me as if I were an intruder. I supposed in their iced-over world I was an unwelcome sight.

"Sorry," I mumbled when I passed an exceptionally noisy group.

"Or would that be a gaggle?" I said to myself, smiling at my own random musings.

Suddenly, to my utter shock and surprise, someone answered.

"That would indeed be a gaggle, Miss Vaughn," a smooth male voice replied.

I spun to face whoever had snuck up on me. However, I knew before I turned around whom I'd find standing there. I knew not just from the voice, a voice I missed, but from the *presence* I felt.

"Lucien," I whispered, "you're here."

I smiled, and he smiled back at me, as dashing as ever. He was bundled up in a long black overcoat and a gray wool scarf. His dark hair was a little mussed and slightly longer than usual, making him look wild and untamed.

"Dahlia," he said, my name rolling off his tongue deliciously, like the day he'd first uttered it.

Oh, how I burned for this man. I longed to tell him how much I had missed him, but there was no need.

"I missed you, too," he quietly replied.

"This is crazy," I said as I stood there and simply stared at him.

He threw back his head and laughed. "Indeed, it is." He offered me his arm. "Come, Dahlia, walk with me."

When I touched him, looping my arm through his, it felt as if I'd come home. Relaxed in a way I'd not known in months, I leaned into him. "Are you mad I'm here?" I asked.

"No," was his simple reply.

And then we walked in silence. We continued in the direction I'd been heading, to the north end of the lake. And as I'd anticipated, Lucien's looming stone mansion was completely visible from that vantage point. What I hadn't anticipated, though, was the perfectly cleared trail leading to his home.

"Is that where you came from?" I asked, looking up at Lucien as we came to a stop.

His dark eyes met mine. "I came from behind you," he reminded me. "If I'd taken the trail, you would have seen me heading in your direction."

I had no response other than, "Good point."

A beat passed, and then I asked, "Where do we go from here, Lucien?"

My question was laden with double meaning.

We resumed walking, and he chuckled. "That depends on you, Dahlia."

"Me?"

"Yes, you." His tone implied, *now sit with that.*

As we neared the cleared trail, I asked, "So, where are we heading right now?"

"To my house, if that's okay with you."

Was he kidding? "Of course it's okay with me," I replied.

Confused, however, I halted my steps. When Lucien did the same, I said, "Just one thing."

"Yes?"

Shifting from foot to foot, I said softly, "I thought we were done, Lucien. I never heard from you after you got the picture back. I figured that was it. It's been more than two months, and I know you've been with other women." I gasped in a breath, the air a cold knife in my lungs. "There's no use pretending. I know you've moved on."

Lucien touched my arm gently. "Dahlia, Dahlia," he murmured.

"What?" I looked up at him. "Did you even hear a single word I just said? You've given me every indication to think we are over and done."

"Yes, I suppose I have."

"Two months," I stressed. "And not one word."

"I'm sorry," he sighed. "I suppose I view time differently. And maybe that part of us, those few days we shared, *is* over." He smiled, as radiant as ever. "But no one ever said there can't be a new beginning, right?"

With that possibility out there, I smiled back at him.

We resumed walking, walking toward his home, walking toward a new, undefined future. Where it would take us, I had no clue.

But it didn't matter.

I was with Lucien now. And whether it was for an hour, a year, or an eternity, I was game for whatever length of time we might have together. Together—as we were meant to be.

Or so I hoped.

Read on for a preview of the next installment of the
Laid Bare novellas,

Unveiled: **LAID BARE**
(Laid Bare Volume #2)

Unveiled: LAID BARE

chapter ONE

Dahlia

Lucien Chambers led me along the icy trail back to his mansion, a Tudor monstrosity that loomed like a ghostly specter on this cold March day. I shivered and quaked in my winter boots. I hoped Lucien couldn't feel my uncertainty, my fear, as it was certainly possible with my arm looped through his.

Whether my sudden trepidation was brought on by anticipation of what would come next, or by outright terror, I couldn't be sure. See, the problem was for as much as I longed to be with Lucien — and oh, did I ever — a part of me feared him. I feared the unknown surrounding him, I feared not knowing *what* he really was, and I feared just how insanely connected to him I felt.

This might not end well. I had to accept that possibility.

A shudder ran through me, prompting Lucien to ask, "Are you having second thoughts, Dahlia?"

I shook my head firmly. "No," I replied.

Lucien slowed up. He spun me to him and cocked his head, assessing me. I smiled up at him. Damn, he was tall.

I guess he saw through my forced ease…or maybe he read my mind, since he said, "We can always turn around, you know."

His voice was smooth and low and I couldn't discern how serious he was.

"I'll walk you back to your car if you want," he continued. "You can return to your apartment, continue on as you have. It will be as if we never came upon one another over by the lake. Whatever you want, Dahlia, I will do…for you."

He gestured to the frozen body of water now in the distance. We'd walked quite far already, closer and closer to the point of no return. "Do you want to go back?" he asked once more, this time only as a whisper.

Lucien clearly wanted me to stay, continue on with him. Swallowing hard, I replied, "I can't go back, Lucien. You know I can't just turn around and leave."

He had this hold over me, and it felt stronger than ever now that we had reunited. He knew this, he had to.

"I do," he replied softly, a response to my thoughts that he could hear when he so desired.

I started to turn away, but I wasn't sure which way to go — back to the car, or to Lucien's.

He grabbed my hand, making my decision for me. I was going nowhere until he'd said his piece.

"Listen to me, Dahlia," he implored. "I can do more than make it as if you never saw me out here today." He lowered his voice and his slight British accent became more pronounced. "I can give you a memory that will leave you thinking you drove up to the park to get away for an afternoon. You'll forget you ran into me, you'll forget all of this. But more than that, I can remove every memory you have of me."

"What?" I was horrified. I wrenched my hand from his, and gasped, "Why would you offer to do such a thing, Lucien? Is that what *you* really want?"

"No," he said, his angry dark eyes meeting my own unhappy stare. "If *I* wanted that I would have left you be over at the lake."

"So, why are you giving me an out? You sought me out."

His eyes penetrating, he murmured. "Yes, I did

seek you out. I sensed your presence, and I came to you. And that is precisely the reason why I am now giving you, as you so eloquently put it, an out."

I smiled, this time genuinely. But Lucien's frown remained, furrowing his raven brows. He had no idea how unearthly beautiful he was, especially at times such as these, when he allowed me to see his vulnerability, his frustration. Usually Lucien was well-aware of his effect on the people around him, particularly me, but I could see how in this moment he had no idea just how incredibly appealing he was.

"What?" he asked, head cocked slightly to the right.

I reached up and swept back an unruly lock of raven-black hair that had fallen to his forehead. "You're beautiful," I said, smiling. "And your accent, it becomes more pronounced when you're worked up over something."

Sighing, he said, "Well, you certainly have the ability to work me up, Dahlia. Don't you?"

Lucien's momentary lapse of control, so unlike him, betrayed how frazzled he was. It was uncharacteristic of him, but so very endearing. His frailties, if you could call them that, made him more human-like. Quite a feat, considering I *knew* he was something far more than merely human.

"I do work you up," I teased, nudging him with my shoulder as I slid my hands into the pockets of my coat. "But I don't do it on purpose."

Lucien had once told me I was his weakness. Now I clearly saw that was true. There was some part of him, like in me, that could not bear to let go.

Knowing that made it easy to say, "I don't want to go back to my car, Lucien. I don't want you to make me forget about anything that happened today. And I definitely don't want an out. I want to remember everything that has ever happened between us."

His brow shot up. "Everything, Dahlia?"

His tone was light. Lucien Chambers was actually engaging in flirtatious banter. I knew then that we had a real chance at something special.

"Yes. I wouldn't give up a single memory, not one moment we've shared."

"Good," he replied, shooting me a dashing smile. "Since I never had any intention of letting you go so easily, anyway."

"Oh, really?" I took a step back.

He took a step forward, and retorted, "Yes, Dahlia, *really*."

I gestured to the trail. I was intrigued, I was thrilled. I threw caution to the wind. Living recklessly had never felt so good as I said, "Let's get going then."

Lucien took my hand. "Wise choice," he murmured.

We began to walk again toward the mansion, and the craziest thing was I could have sworn I heard Lucien mutter under his breath, "Although a choice was never an option anyway."

What that meant, I couldn't begin to imagine.

But I couldn't wait to find out.

Unveiled: Laid Bare (Volume 2) ~ **available June 2015.** *Unveiled* **will contain Dahlia's point-of-view, and due to popular demand Lucien will be heard, as well.**

ACKNOWLEDGEMENTS

The biggest "thank you" goes out to the readers. Thank you for taking a chance on this departure for me. I am learning novellas are their own brand of special. It's fun to dole out a little bit of a larger story one bit at a time. I hope you'll be brave and stick with me throughout Lucien and Dahlia's story. I think you'll enjoy their journey.

As always, thank you to family, friends, bloggers, and the most awesome street team ever. Much appreciation also goes out to Hot Tree Editing, Cover It! Designs, and the formatting team at E.M. Tippetts.

Thank you!!!

ABOUT THE AUTHOR

S.R. Grey is an Amazon Top 100 and Barnes & Noble Top #1 Bestselling author. She is the author of the popular Judge Me Not series, the Inevitability duology, A Harbour Falls Mystery trilogy, and the new series of Laid Bare novellas. Ms. Grey's works have appeared on Amazon Bestseller lists and Barnes & Noble Bestseller lists in multiple categories.

Ms. Grey resides in Pennsylvania. When not writing, Ms. Grey can be found reading, traveling, running, or cheering for her hometown sports teams.

Author Website:
http://srgrey.com/

S.R. Grey Facebook:
http://www.facebook.com/pages/SR-Grey/361159217278943

Sign up for S.R. Grey's exclusive-content newsletter and never miss an update, cover reveal, or release:
http://mad.ly/signups/106801/join

**Read the first chapter of S.R. Grey's newest New
Adult/Romantic Suspense novel,** *Inevitable Detour*

INEVITABLE DETOUR

Chapter One

I stare at the computer screen. It's my last exam of spring semester, and there are only five questions left on the Strategic Management final before me.

My eyes are glued to words, forming a single question. I know the answer. Yes, I do. But then my vision blurs, and I think, *ugh, whose idea was it for me to major in business?*

Not mine.

The cursor on the screen blinks over answer choice B. Like I said, I know the correct answer, and it sure as hell isn't B.

What to do…what to do…

With a sly grin, I choose B and hit next.

I am feeling particularly defiant today. My parents left me a voice mail this morning, telling me in no uncertain terms that any thoughts of heading up to New York City this summer with my best friend and roommate, Haven Shaw, are best put to rest. So much for thinking it'd be fun to hang out in the Big Apple with Haven while she worked on finding an agent, making acting contacts, and generally just doing whatever it is a person needs to do when preparing to land a part in a play someday.

And not just any play.

"Broadway, here I come," Haven said the other day when we were discussing her big-city dreams.

She's a bit theatrical, but that's to be expected. She's a theater major, after all. Her goal is to eventually make it as an actress on the Great White Way.

Conversely, my dreams are much smaller. My primary longing lately is for something — *anything* — to happen in my mundane life. I thought New York would be a promising start. Guess not. Thanks to my parents and their aversion to anything fun for Essa, there will be no excitement in my life this summer. Nope. Just like the two previous summers, I'll be lulling away the time here at Oakwood College. Excitement for me will consist of chilling in the coffee shop on the edge of the tiny Pennsylvania town my small college is located in. My after-class afternoons will include exciting activities like staring out at cows and farmland, sipping on a mocha, and wishing and hoping for something more.

And that's just not right.

I'm a damn straight-A student, for God's sake. I don't need to spend the summer at Oakwood, taking stupid summer classes. Unfortunately, my parents don't care about my wants and needs. They believe their only child should apply herself year-round. Forget that I'm already a model daughter.

Well, more or less. But that's neither here nor there.

Bottom line is that my parents will not, as they put it in their terse message, have me "veering off course."

Oh, really? So they think...

My defiance hits full throttle, and I purposely choose the wrong answers for the next four questions.

I hit submit and think, *take that, Mr. and Mrs. Brant.*

Despite my actions, I'll still receive a solid A for the class. My GPA will not suffer in the slightest. Still, it feels kind of good to be bad.

That's sad, Essa, that choosing a few wrong answers on a final is the best defiant act you can come up with.

Sighing, I click a button to indicate I am finished with the exam. I then grab my purse from the back of the chair and head for the door. "You're pathetic," I mumble to myself as I step out into a warm, stuffy hallway that smells of varnish and books.

I kind of like the smell as it wraps around me. It's the smell of students seeking knowledge; it's the smell of youth. Despite all my protestations to the contrary,

I do like college. I would just prefer to be studying something of my own choosing.

I stand and ponder. Not only does the smell of school envelope me, but the heat of the day does as well. The second-floor hall I'm lingering in is about ten degrees warmer than the classroom was. Dropping my purse to the floor, I shrug out of my olive-green mock-army jacket. I'm down to two layered tanks, blue over white, but I am still roasting.

"Blech," I pant, fanning myself as I bend down to pick up my purse. The button on my pants threatens to pop, and I let out a curse. I really should have worn a pair of nice, loose shorts instead of squeezing my ass into overly stylish skinny jeans this morning.

Maybe if the jeans were a little looser, I'd be more comfy.

I do a funny little dance in the thankfully empty area outside the classroom. Sadly, the jeans don't feel a single inch looser. Damn designers. Don't they realize we're not all model-perfect? When I exhale, the button squeezes once again at my middle, and I remind myself that I need to lay off the sweets.

Yeah, right. A girl has to have some kind of indulgence, right? And since I'm no exception, sugary treats are it for me. Otherwise, I'm fairly straight and narrow. I don't do drugs, and I don't smoke. I also barely drink — two drinks are my limit when I do imbibe — and I'm not promiscuous.

"Far from it," I mumble.

I've only had sex once, in fact. And what a disaster *that* turned out to be. The memory alone, from one of the few nights I deviated from my two-drinks policy, at a Saint Patrick's Day party two months ago, leaves me feeling nauseated. Yeah, the thirty seconds spent with the senior who was cowriting an article with me for the online *Oakwood College Gazette* just wasn't worth the time it took to take off my clothes. All too clearly, a fuzzy memory of him grunting on top of me, sweaty and harsh, comes to mind. I kept regretting that this was how I was losing my virginity. I still regret it. But what can you do? Last time I checked there were no time machines.

So, yeah, forget about sex. That's my motto. I'll stick with sugar-laden goodies for now. Like cupcakes. Haven made a batch to celebrate our surviving finals week. Her homemade buttercream frosting is far better than sex any day. Not to mention it's more orgasm-inducing than the thirty seconds that had me asking, "What? That's it? Why bother?"

I sigh. I need to get back to the apartment and hit up those awesome cupcakes. But my feet are far from moving. I can't believe I daydreamed away five whole minutes. Or maybe it's been ten.

Retrieving my phone from my purse, I send Haven a quick text: *Leaving Byers Hall. Don't eat all the cupcakes.*

A few seconds later, she texts back: *Oops. I got hungry and ate the rest for dinner. Sorry.*

Bitch, I reply.

Whore, is her response.

I call her a bitch again and laugh. She's laughing too. I'm sure of it. Haven knows my texts are sent with love. She is so not a bitch, and I would never think such a thing for real. Nor do I suspect she sees me as a whore. I am far from it, as established. Well, unless we're talking sugar. Then, I'm a full-blown slut.

Haven sends another text. *Just kidding, Es. I didn't eat all the cupcakes. I know you love them, so I left the rest for you.*

Aww, Haven is the best. *You're super sweet*, I text back, and then I start down the hallway. Finally.

As I amble along, I think of how Haven is definitely one of the better parts of my life. Throughout the course of the past three years, we've become best friends. We met at a freshman orientation. It was an early one, held during the spring prior to matriculation. We sat next to each other and clicked immediately, which is kind of amusing, since we're so different from one another.

Somehow, though, we just work. Bottom line, I love Haven, and I'd do anything for her. She's certainly done some selfless things for me, no doubt about that. As a result, we're close, thicker than thieves some say. I tease Haven all the time; tell her she's my sister from another mother. Since her own mom passed away years ago, she usually replies that she'd let my mom adopt her. But then she adds the qualifier, "that is, if she wasn't so damn overbearing."

Understatement of the year.

Just the other day, after I received a call from my mom — she was checking in on my studying — Haven joked, "If your mom took me in she'd probably insist I change my major from theater to business."

"She probably would," I agreed.

It's true. My mother means well, as does my dad, but both my parents have a tendency to focus on practicality. And to the Mr. and Mrs. Brant, practicality means majoring in business.

"It's always smart to major in something marketable," Dad likes to say.

"Like business, honey," Mom always adds with a smile. "You're making smart choices, Essa."

Too bad they're not *my* choices.

Wishing I was more like Haven, who answers to no one, I round the corner and run smack dab into one of Haven's acting professors. To my dismay, it's the shitty professor who broke my friend's heart two weeks ago.

"Hi, Essa," Professor Walsh says cordially while pretending to step out of my path.

He remains in the way, of course. Still, I manage to slip around him. He nonetheless stays with me, turning and watching me the whole time.

Ugh. It is so hard not to snipe, "Get the hell out of my face, you fucking douche bag."

Since I lack the courage to say such a thing, I hold my tongue.

But when Professor Walsh reaches out and touches my arm, halting my progress, I twist from his grasp and snap, "Really?" I raise both brows and take a step back. "Please tell me you did not just lay your hand on me."

"Now, now," Douche Bag Walsh says in a sickly, patronizing tone. "There's no need for such a venomous retort. I don't know what Haven has told you —"

"Try everything," I interrupt.

Haven and her thirty-five-year-old professor had a three-month fling. It was all hot and heavy, not to mention illicit as hell, until he ended it in a not-so-nice way.

Concern fills the professor's light-brown eyes as he taps his foot and stares at me. It's not concern for the girl whose heart he's broken. It's purely concern for his own ass. Oh, the trouble he could get into for fucking one of his students.

"Don't worry," I say, just to get him to stop staring and, hopefully, go away. "Haven won't let me go to the disciplinary board, and God knows she'll never do it herself, so your secret is safe."

The professor, more confident as soon as he hears I plan to keep my mouth shut, lazily brushes back a lock of wispy, dirty-blond hair that's fallen to his forehead. He's boyishly handsome, and this is a move he's obviously perfected.

Too bad it does absolutely nothing for me.

Undeterred, he says in a low voice, "Everything that happened between me and Haven Shaw was consensual. She's twenty-two years old, Miss Brant. Last time I checked that makes her an adult."

I feel like screaming in his smug face. "You were her freaking professor, prick. Not only did you violate school policy, but you violated her when you let her fall in love with you and then callously walked away."

But there's no point in lashing out. Haven is still hung up on the guy, shady though he is. She doesn't want him to get into any trouble. And someone might hear me if I start going off in defense of my friend. The halls are empty, but many of the classrooms are full.

So I don't say a thing. I do, however, scowl at the man. And then I walk away, leaving him standing in the middle of the hall. I feel his eyes on me, probably checking out my ass. His hooking up with Haven wasn't some fluke. It's common knowledge that Professor Walsh has a thing for college-age girls. Until Haven, he was known as a one-and-done kind of guy. But he was really into Haven, for a while… until he wasn't.

It's really no surprise he liked her as much as he did in the early days of their fling. Men find Haven irresistible. And why wouldn't they? The girl is gorgeous. She is far prettier than I am. Haven is tall, with a model-like body. I am short, not super thin. Haven has big, expressive aquamarine eyes and shiny, raven-black hair. I have boring hair that can't even decide what color it wants to be. Some days it appears light brown, other days it's more of a dark blonde shade. Not that I pay much notice. I usually just pile the long, unruly tresses up in a sloppy bun, or twist the mess into a ponytail.

I'm not saying I'm unattractive. I just don't really

stand out in a crowd. Not like Haven does.

Despite all she has going for her, Haven is far from conceited. She's unassuming and genuine, loyal to the core. That's why I maintain that she didn't deserve to be treated the way Professor Walsh treated her. He used her for sex, strung her along, and then unceremoniously dumped her with no explanation two weeks ago.

My ire at the jerk professor escalates. By the time I reach the stairs, I am smacking my hand down on the dark wood railing in anger. Quickly, I spin around, intent on stomping back and having one last word with the guy.

But he's long gone.

"Chickenshit," I murmur.

Sighing, I step over to a wall and lean back against it. There's a classroom a few feet away, in session. Leaning my head back, I listen to the soothing murmur of voices, thus allowing myself a few minutes to calm down.

Soon, I am relaxed. I also find I am fully engaged in listening to the lecture. Not surprising since the instructor, her voice light and feminine, is speaking on a subject I find fascinating—the role of fate in our lives. I walk over to the door and press my ear up against it.

"Wonderful," she says. "You've all shared some great insights. But now that we've dissected Shakespeare's use of fate in *Romeo and Juliet* and *Macbeth*, I have a question for you, a question regarding *your* lives."

The class titters, she chuckles, and I step back to where I'm able to lean against the wall. After a minute or two, I slide down to a seated position.

"What I want to know," the instructor continues, "is who here believes that real lives—*our* lives—are influenced by fate?"

"I do," I whisper. *At least I think I do.*

The professor calls on someone in the class, a girl. She responds, "I believe all of our lives are influenced by fate. And I firmly believe in destiny."

"Is there a difference?" the instructor questions.

The girl replies, "Yes, I think so. I've always heard that fate refers to the bad things that happen in our lives."

"And destiny?" the instructor prompts.

"It's the good stuff."

"That is a commonly accepted belief," the instructor concurs.

There's some shuffling of papers.

"What it all comes down to," the instructor continues, "is that every person's life is destined for a certain path. We may not realize it, especially when it's happening, but we *will* end up where we're supposed to be."

Wow. I think about my own life. I believe in concepts like fate and destiny. But, to my chagrin, I don't feel as if either has ever touched my life. In some ways, I suppose my parents have prevented *things* from happening by the way they've structured everything for me. Still, I hold out hope that something that is "meant to be" will eventually occur. If that doesn't happen, what will become of me? My biggest fear is that I'll graduate from college next year — with my shiny, new business degree — and move right back to my hometown of Philadelphia. Maybe I'll become an accountant, like my mom and dad. And maybe, like Mom and Dad, I'll never really *live*.

"Ugh." I place my face in my hands. I don't want to be an accountant. I'd rather eat pocket lint, I swear. If I had my way, I'd much rather work as a writer, a journalist of some sort. I find joy in writing articles for the school paper. But, really, if I dare to dream big, I see myself as an investigative journalist. The kind that seeks out exciting stories, stories with an element of danger.

Who in the hell am I kidding? I'm play-it-by the-rules Essa Brant. "Let's be real here," I whisper.

Sighing, I return my attention to the instructor and her big words on fate.

"Remember," she says. Her tone is so very serious, so very ominous. "Just because you think fate or destiny hasn't yet guided your life in some noticeable way doesn't mean it won't happen. I promise you, my friends, you will end up where you're supposed to be. And how can I say that with such certainty? The answer is simple: You can't escape your destiny."

Okay, so where will fate lead me? What is my destiny?

On a roll, the instructor goes on. "Things happen in our lives that are predetermined, whether we realize it or not. Often it's a series of small events that slowly and methodically lead us to where we're supposed to be. But sometimes it's a big, cataclysmic event that changes the course of everything. Even so, you may not realize your life is changing at the time. Something may happen to someone you know, perhaps someone close to you. Their 'something' ends up affecting you. *Your* life is now altered; *you're* set on a different path." The instructor pauses, and then she says, "Think of this path as an inevitable detour of sorts."

Everyone in the classroom is so quiet you'd hear a pin drop if someone were inclined to drop one. Guess everyone is deep in thought, wondering what "inevitable detour" is in store for them. And how will this "detour" alter their lives. God knows that's what I'm thinking.

"We have about ten minutes left," the instructor announces, breaking the trance she was holding everyone in, including me. "Are there any questions, class?"

A lively Q&A ensues, and I know it's high time I get up off my ass and go home. But I can't leave, not yet. I need a minute to take in all I've heard. It's like when someone puts something in your head, and that's all you think about. Now, I can't help but imagine an inevitable detour of my own. Maybe I should take charge and make one happen next week. I could defy my parents and go to New York City with Haven. It might be worth my parents' ire to finally venture out of the only state I've ever known. Not only would my bestie and I have a great time tearing up the town, but I'd be staying with Haven in her older brother's apartment. And there's a good chance that though Farren Shaw travels a lot for some crazy-secretive job he has, I'd finally have an opportunity to meet him. Possibly, I could even spend some time with him.

Gah. A thrill shoots through me at the thought of spending even a mere minute with Farren. Now there's an inevitable detour I'd like to take. Much like his sister, Farren is gorgeous. He has the same raven-black hair, same model-perfect features, like full lips and high cheekbones. His eyes, however, are not aquamarine. They're better; they're a unique and stunning shade of green. Not that I've had the pleasure of viewing these stunning green eyes in person. Only in pictures have I seen them, since, sadly, I've never actually met Farren. He's not around much. He was in the military for years, special ops according to Haven. And though he was discharged over a year ago, he still spends a good deal of time in other countries for his "work." Consequently, he's never visited Oakwood College campus. That's why I've never met him. And that is why I'm so incredibly upset about New York. That would have been my chance. Travel or no, he'd have to stop home at some point.

Oh well. Guess I'll have to continue to rely on pictures and short videos of Haven's incredibly handsome brother to fuel my libido. And by fuel, I mean on all cylinders. I may not have much of an interest in sex, but I am still a woman. And, as a woman, I sense a man like Farren could change my mind on the sex-thing. He's like some dream guy — tall, dark, and too handsome for words.

So, yeah, I'm into him. It's mostly a secret, though. However, I must confess that once, several months ago, Haven caught me uploading pictures of Farren from her computer to my phone.

"Cyberstalking my brother, I see," she teased as she walked over to where I was seated—rather uneasily at that point—on the sofa in our living room, her laptop in my hands.

"No, no," I stammered while trying to close all the open windows…of Farren in uniform, Farren standing next to Haven, and Farren—a recent shot— in a finely tailored suit.

"He does look good in that one," she said, tapping the screen before the picture of her brother in a dark suit disappeared.

She was right. Farren in a business suit was all kinds of serious hot, so I had to agree. Then, I turned from the computer and asked, "Does he have to wear suits for his new job?"

She shrugged. "I don't know, Essa. I guess."

"What exactly *is* his new job?" I pressed. "You said he's some kind of personal security contractor, right? What does that mean, exactly?"

"I don't really know," Haven admitted. Then, with a laugh, she said, "All I know is whatever Farren does he gets paid a lot of money."

"I hope it's nothing illegal," I mumbled under my breath.

Hey, it's not so farfetched to think such a thing. Not only does Farren fund his sister's college education — as well as all her expenses — but he also has plenty of money for himself. He owns some of the best real estate in the world, including a luxurious New York City apartment. The place is sweet, very sweet, located on the Upper West Side of Manhattan, in a high-rise building right next to Central Park. I've seen pictures, and it looks like the kind of place a celebrity would live in. Not that I care about the money Farren has, but the fact that he has so much of it does make me curious.

See, Farren and Haven Shaw were not born into any kind of money, not like the level of wealth Farren currently possesses. Their childhood circumstances were far from ideal and not anywhere near upscale. Their dad, a man named Alan Shaw, disappeared, seemingly into thin air, when they were very young. At the time, Farren was ten and Haven was only three. Their mom was left to struggle on her own to support her two young children. And she was doing okay, until she was killed in a car crash. Seventeen-year-old Farren and ten-year-old Haven were sent to live with their aunt — someone who absolutely did not want the burden of her sister's kids. Her aunt was cold and indifferent. Haven has said many times that her aunt was far from nice. That's why Farren joined the army the day he turned eighteen. He left and started sending Haven money right away. Their aunt was always cheap with them, buying the kids only the bare essentials. Despite all of those things, to this day, Haven still craves family. She tries so hard to maintain a relationship with her aunt. But the woman rarely — if ever — returns Haven's calls.

My phone vibrates, bringing me back to the present. It's another text from Haven.

Where are you? You better get your ass home soon. We're still going out tonight, right?

Of course, I type back. *I haven't forgotten that we're celebrating the fact we survived our third year of college.*

We did, didn't we?

Hell, yeah, I type back. *Seniors next year. Woohoo.*

I'll drink to that, Haven replies.

Me, too.

Hey, by the way, I hope you're planning on having more than two beers tonight. Rules are out the window.

Ha-ha. And, yes, rules are out the window.

Good, she texts. *Who knows, Essa, maybe you'll get so loosened up that you'll end up meeting your fantasy man.*

If only she knew it's her brother who stars in my fantasies. Just thinking about the man — and he is a man, not some fumbling college boy — gets me all worked up. But it's ridiculous to continue on like this. I'll surely never meet Farren, seeing as New York City is off the table.

Resigned to live my parent-directed life, which certainly does not include hot guys, I push all thoughts of my secret fantasy, Farren Shaw, to the back of my mind. Gathering up my purse, I stand. But before I leave, I think about the lecture I listened in on.

Fate…

Destiny…

What's in store for me? Where will these so-called predetermined events lead me? Somewhere, everywhere, nowhere. The possibilities are endless. Still, I have to wonder if there will ever be an inevitable detour in *my* life.

"Yeah, right," I quietly scoff. The only inevitability in my future is that my life will continue as planned. But the instructor's words resonate in my head, reminding me that we can't escape our destiny and that we always end up where we're supposed to be.

Of course, for that to happen, it may require a bit more defiance on my part. Particularly when it comes to my parents and where they expect me to spend this summer.

Good, okay. That's fine with me.

'Cause I think I'm finally ready to start pressing B every chance I get.

Continue the story…

Available on Amazon, Barnes & Noble, and ITunes

Read the prologue of *I Stand Before You*, the first novel in S.R. Grey's Judge Me Not series.

I STAND BEFORE YOU

Prologue
Chase

I lean my head back against the headrest, crank the passenger window down the rest of the way. The June night air rustles through my hair, reminding me I desperately need a trim. I run my fingers through the strands, chasing the path of the breeze.

My grandmother likes to lecture that I shouldn't have hair sticking out at odd angles, strands curling at the nape of my neck.

"You're such a handsome young man, Chase," Grandma Gartner said just this morning, *tsk*ing when I sat down for breakfast. "You look so much like your father did when he was your age. But, you know, *he* always kept *his* hair short and tidy." And then there was a pause, a long, dramatic sigh. She set down a plate of eggs—over easy—in front of me. "My poor Jack. God rest his soul." My grandmother crossed herself.

Her poor Jack, my father with the short and tidy hair—dead and gone.

I thought: *I am not my dad, Gram. He failed us, he gave up on us.* But the words never passed my lips. And they never will. Hearing them would only hurt my grandmother's feelings and she's too good to hear the angry thoughts poisoning my polluted mind. So I keep all that shit locked deep inside.

This morning was no different. I kept things light, said something like, "The girls like my hair like this, Gram. Got to keep the ladies happy, ya know."

Then I ducked and waited for the inevitable swat with the dish towel. But it never came. Instead, the lines in my grandmother's face deepened.

"You don't need to be concerning yourself with keeping ladies happy, young man. You're only twenty. Messing with women at your age will only lead to trouble."

I knew what she meant this morning, and I know it now too. She's worried I'll end up getting some girl pregnant. Then I'll be fucked, well and good. But I'm always careful, take the necessary precautions. Besides, it isn't my womanizing ways that's becoming a problem. If only. No, unfortunately, it's my ever-growing dependency on drugs—something my grandmother would never suspect—that has me worried these days.

These days... Yeah, right. More like these blurry,

fucked-up segments of time.

Sighing, I roll the window up just enough to lean my head against the cool glass. *What am I going to do?* I silently ask myself.

What I really need to do is get the hell out of this tiny Ohio farm town I landed back in two years ago. I'm spinning my wheels here in Harmony Creek, hanging with a bad crowd. Problem is I have no plan, no money either. Drugs are my escape and have been for quite a while. My priorities are all fucked up. My life, it's upside down. Every day it seems like getting high — and staying that way — is my only goal. I want to stop — believe me I do — but I don't think I know how to anymore.

A lump forms in my throat at this thought, but I swallow it down. "Hey," I say to Tate, who is driving. "Let's get out of this town."

Tate Cody, my friend...and my partner in crime in everything wild and crazy these days — women, drugs, drinking, fighting — you name it, we do it. And if we're not doing it nowadays, chances are we've done it at least once over the past couple of years. We've yet to slow down; we live on the edge.

I sometimes wonder when we'll fall.

"What do you think we're doing, Chase, my man?"

I take in and process Tate's reply, while he lifts a bottle of cheap gin to his lips and hits the gas. And for this one long, tortuous drawn-out second, I can't make a distinction between what I asked Tate and what I was only thinking. I panic, assuming my partner in crime's response is to let me know it's finally happening, we're really falling.

But then Tate adds, "I'm getting us out of here as fast as I can," and I breathe a little easier. He just means we're leaving Harmony Creek. Not falling, after all. *Shit, I need to ease up on the drugs.*

I glance out the window, and though it's dark I can see we're heading east, nearing the state line. Soon we'll be out of Ohio completely, and in the neighboring state of Pennsylvania. That's where we're supposed to hook up with two girls tonight. They're from New Castle, and we're meeting at a lake across the state line.

I don't really care about all that, though. What I'd really rather do is keep on going. Hop on Interstate 80 and clock the miles to Jersey. Better yet, Tate and I could go farther. We could drive our asses straight into New York-fucking-City. Now that would be sweet.

So while Tate barrels down a back road the police rarely patrol—until you get into Pennsylvania, that is — I pretend we're leaving Harmony Creek for good. No looking back, no regrets, just flying the fuck out of this lame-ass small town.

And speaking of flying, I'm flying a bit now too, feeling fine, baby, fine. I close my eyes so I can savor the s-l-o-w creep of numbness that cocoons me like a warm and fuzzy blanket.

I feel nothing, yet I feel everything.

My skin tingles a little, but when I touch my hand to my face it feels detached, like these parts of my body belong to two different people, neither of them me. That thought makes me happy, escape is exactly what I crave.

Needless to say, I've smoked — a lot — and not just weed. But it's the pills I swallowed a while ago that are starting to wrap me up and spin me the fuck out.

A bottle hits the back of my hand and my eyes fly open. Shit, I forgot I am not alone in this car.

"Drink, fucker," Tate urges.

I take the gin, despite the fact I can barely see straight. *No* isn't part of my vocabulary when I'm like this. And, sadly, more often than not, this is exactly how I am. This is who I am becoming: Chase Gartner, burgeoning drug addict.

As per most nights, Tate and I stopped at Kyle's before embarking on *this* night's little adventure. Kyle

Tanner supplies us with more drugs than we could ever hope for. And the quality is always top notch. Kyle takes a certain kind of pride in dealing only primo product. But you'd never guess such a thing if you saw the rundown shithole he lives in.

Our dealer resides on the *other* side of town, over by the closed-down glass factory, in a clapboard house he shares with his meth-addicted dad. Lately, going there has been a contradiction of emotions for me. I love and hate concurrently when Tate and I cross over the railroad tracks that mark the end of the safe neighborhoods of Harmony Creek. Then, I vacillate between love and hate as I watch the Sparkle Mart grocery store appear…then disappear. I lean a little more towards hate when we reach the rundown apartment building where the junkies hang out, where their emaciated bodies lean lazily against the dirty brick exterior.

I sure as fuck don't want to end up there, God, no. But maybe I'm powerless to stop my downward spiral. Lord knows, by the time we start down the long dirt road that leads to Kyle's place, I crave and I want. And love trumps hate by that point. Even the junkies seem less scary. So we go…and we go…and we keep going back.

Tate tells me the road to Kyle's house is the road

to salvation. *Salvation, my ass.* I'd be more inclined to say Tate and I are traveling a path to hell. We're in the express lane to damnation, and one step closer to burning every time we travel down that fucking dirt road. I know it, he knows it, but do we ever do anything to stop? Do we try to crawl out of the hole we're wallowing in? No, never.

In fact, Tate wants us to delve in deeper — start selling. He says we'll make, at the minimum, enough money to help pay for the copious amounts of shit we ingest…snort…smoke. Yeah, we do it all, everything short of needles. I somehow know if I ever cross *that* line, there will be no going back.

But I'm considering the selling thing, albeit for a different reason than my friend. Tate hopes to eventually make enough cash to buy his own wheels. He hates borrowing the piece of shit we're currently in — his mom's old, rusted Ford Focus. I just want to make enough money to buy a ticket out of this place. The little bit I earn painting people's houses, picking up construction work here and there — it's not adding up fast enough for my liking.

Hell, I still live at my grandmother's farmhouse out on Cold Springs Lane. Granted, I recently fixed up the little apartment above the detached garage, moved from a bedroom in the main house to an area not too much larger. But that little apartment provides privacy, and that's what I need. I am no longer a teenager, like when I first moved back two years ago. That's why I want, more than anything, to just get the fuck out of here. I'm thinking the money I make selling will make escape a reality, not just some pipe dream. No pun intended.

I raise the bottle of gin to my lips and tip it back. Alcohol heats my throat. "I think I'm going to take Kyle up on his offer," I say after I swallow the burn, the resulting grimace distorting my voice. "I need the money and it's going to take forever to earn it legit."

"You're making the right decision, my friend," Tate replies as he reaches over to take back the bottle.

Whoa… My vision turns wonky. There are three overlapping filmy images of my friend, and then just two.

"It's all about the numbers, man," two filmy Tates tell me.

I tell myself I need to slow down, and then I say to Tate, "That it is." I squeeze my eyes shut to keep from swaying in my seat. "That it is," I repeat.

The irony is that I once had money. Well, my family did, enough that my parents had a trust fund set up for me. Not a big one, mind you, but enough that it would've allowed for me to go to a decent college, get set up in a new city, shit like that.

I have no idea what my future holds nowadays, but I know it's been tainted by my past.

Back when I was around eight my parents moved from this town out to Las Vegas. My dad, who'd been successfully building houses here for a while, started a similar construction business out in Nevada. The timing was right, the stars aligned. We caught magic in the early days of the housing boom. Everything was golden and money poured in. It was happy times. For a while.

During those good times, Mom got pregnant. She gave me a little brother named Will that I still love like crazy and miss every fucking day. We used to talk on the phone all the time, but now I'm lucky if I get a two-word text from my little bro. I suppose when you're eleven years old — and haven't seen your big brother in two years — memories become a little hazy.

That's another thing the extra money from selling drugs will help with: I'll have enough funds to fly out to Vegas to see Will. Or I can just buy him a ticket to come here. As it is my mom, Abby, barely makes enough to get by out there.

But, like I said before, it wasn't always that way. In the early years, my father's construction company grew and thrived, so much so that I once entertained dreams of taking over the business. I used to imagine following in my father's footsteps, as sons are apt to do.

One afternoon, when I was about thirteen, I told my dad I wanted to build homes, same as he did. I showed him some sketches, just some basic designs and floor plans I'd thrown together. My dad was impressed. And not the false kind of fawning parents often try to sell to their kids. No, my drawings truly floored Jack Gartner. I could tell he couldn't believe his eldest son possessed that kind of crazy talent. He told me I should aim high, the sky was the limit. My sketches were incredible, he said, especially for my age. I could be an architect if I wanted, design skyscrapers even.

I had no reason not to believe him.

When you're thirteen you think you can have it all. Life hasn't roughed you up so very much…yet. At least it hadn't for me. So I told my father I'd do both—I would design the skyscrapers, and then I'd build them. My buildings would sell like hotcakes, and I'd be as rich as Donald Trump. No, richer even.

"The sky's the limit," I said, echoing my father's words back to him.

Dad smiled and patted me on the back.

Jack Gartner wasn't patronizing me, he truly

believed in my possibility. "You have talent, Chase," he said. "Just don't ever lose yourself. If you can stay true to your dream…to who you are…then you'll do more than fly. Someday you'll soar."

Yeah, right. I sure am soaring at the moment, but I have a feeling this isn't what Dad had in mind.

Tate tries to pass the bottle back to me, but my mood has dampened. The pills, along with the memories, are doing a fucking number on my emotions. I'm sad one minute, reflective the next, mad at everything, contemplative over nothing. I guess I am officially fucked up.

I push the bottle away, harder than necessary, and clear liquid sloshes over the side. "Asshole," Tate mutters.

"Sorry," I say.

Do I really mean it? No, it's just a word, an empty string of letters. Empty, like me.

I tune Tate out. I am high as fuck and lost in my mind. We idle at a swinging red light hanging over an empty, dark stretch of road, and I sit waiting on an imaginary red light in my head, one on memory-fucking-lane.

When I blink, both lights turn green…

My dad started taking me to work the summer I showed him the drawings. I learned how to wire a home, how to put in plumbing, how to lay insulation. And that was just the beginning. I used to watch how my dad talked to the guys. He treated them with respect, and in turn they went the extra mile for him. It was all "Yes sir, Mr. Gartner," "Consider it done, Jack."

When I turned fourteen, my dad bought me a drafting table, a bunch of fancy software too. The kind real architects use, or so he said. I practiced all the time, got pretty damn good. I was building my wings, you see, preparing to fly.

Will was only five, but damn if that kid didn't love to sit around and watch me sketch. For him, I'd draw all kinds of ridiculous structures.

"Dwaw me a house, Chasey," he asked this one day.

I laughed while I tousled his blond hair. I remember the fine strands looked so light in the sunlit room. Hell, they were almost white. "All right, buddy, what kind do you want?"

"A house like a tweeeee," Will sing-song replied, green eyes innocent and wide as he focused on the sketch pad I'd picked up from my desk.

I readied a colored pencil and asked for clarification, "Okay, a tree house, right?"

"No-o-o." Will shook his little head vociferously.

"A house that *is* a twee, Chasey."

"Aha, got it," I said.

And I did. I drew Will a tree house shaped exactly like a tree, big, sturdy, loaded down with bushy branches. The leaves I shaded in the color of my brother's eyes. I sketched a door at the base of the trunk, then drew a Will-sized truck and parked it under a low-lying branch. After I finished with some final shading, I held the drawing up for my brother to see.

Will's house looked like one of those tree houses in the commercials with the elves and the cookies, only this one I'd drawn was far better. There was a lot more detail, and I'd drawn the tree in 2-D. In among the branches and the leaves all the rooms were in cross-section, done up in varying shades of blue, Will's favorite color. I also made certain every last blue-shaded 2D-room overflowed with toys.

Will threw his arms around my neck and told me he loved his *twee house*. Then, he leaned back and told me he loved *me* even more.

He gave me a kiss on my cheek. That shit always touched my heart, choked me up a little. "I love you too, buddy," was about all I could say as I held on to a little boy who meant the world to me.

Things are never bad when love is abundant. I

thought it would stay that way forever, I did. A home filled with love, a happy family, just a good and easy life.

Man, was I ever wrong.

Shortly after I turned seventeen my world began to crumble. The bottom fell out of the housing market. The wave everyone was riding touched the surf and crashed. My dad's business was one of the first to fail. He had overextended himself; all our assets were mortgaged. He made ridiculous deals, attempting to keep us afloat, but his efforts proved futile. We sunk faster than a stone.

I sold the fancy architect software on eBay, the drafting table too. I gave the money to my parents, but it was merely a drop in the bucket compared to what we owed. I watched my once-vibrant dad turn into a shadow of the man he once was. My mom, always so young-looking and pretty, developed dark circles under her eyes—from crying, worrying, not being able to sleep. She even tried her hand at the casinos, we were that fucking desperate. But everyone knows gambling is a loser's game. The house always wins in the end.

One night, my mom was at one of those casinos. It wasn't the first time she'd spent hours and hours away, trying to win back what we'd lost. She came out ahead a little here and there, but it was never enough, never enough.

Will had fallen asleep early that night, so my dad and I were more or less alone. He asked me if I was hungry. When I nodded slowly, reluctant to reveal just how ravenous I really was and cause my father any additional undue guilt, he sighed, picked up the phone, and ordered a bunch of Chinese take-out.

I swear I smelled that food before the delivery man even pulled up to the house. Beef Chow Mein, General Tso's chicken, Hot and Sour soup, and eggrolls, the first real meal I'd eaten in weeks. And even though my dad and I had to sit on the floor — our furniture had been repossessed days earlier — I savored every fucking bite.

Afterward, my dad said he had somewhere to go. There was something he had to do. Would I keep an eye on Will?

"Sure," I told him while shoving white take-out cartons with little metal handles — leftovers I'd saved for Will and Mom — into the fridge.

With my father gone, I had nothing to do. Our TVs were gone, the stereos too. Video games? Forget it. Those were among the first things to go. So, I wandered around the house barefoot, padding around on neglected hardwood floors. I trudged from one empty room to the next.

Then I took a minute to look in on Will.

My little brother slept on an air mattress in the middle of his now-barren room. The *twee house* sketch, the only thing left on his four stark walls, had fallen. It lay abandoned on the floor, close to Will's hand, close to where his little arm was dangling off the side of the mattress. To me, it looked as if my brother was subconsciously reaching for the drawing. Three years had passed since I'd drawn Will's tree house — and I'd sketched hundreds of other things for him since that sunny day — but that particular piece of made-with-love art was still my brother's favorite. I think to him it symbolized something more. He'd once said my sketch gave him hope. I guess it reminded him of when things were good.

I stepped into his dark room and picked up Will's hope. I kissed the top of his head and gently placed his *twee house* next to his sleeping form. I made my way back down to the living room, feeling solemn and too fucking worn for seventeen. Tears welled in my eyes, but I refused to let them fall. *Hell with that shit.* The paper bag that had held the Chinese food was still on the floor. Frustrated, I kicked it out of my way. A fortune cookie shot out and landed at my feet. I picked the projectile up, ripped the plastic covering off, and slid a tiny piece of paper from the confines of the cookie.

The fortune stayed in my hand, the cookie ended up in my mouth.

Truthfully, I was still hungry. Crunching away and savoring sugary goodness, I read the words on the little slip of paper I held between my fingers.

As I stand before you, judge me not.

It sounded a little hokey and I almost threw the fortune away. But there was something about those words that made me hesitate, something almost prescient. I ended up folding the little piece of paper in half and tucking it in to my pocket. Maybe I needed some symbol of hope just like my brother. I knew the things happening in my life would eventually define my future, and I guess I hoped no matter what occurred those things wouldn't ultimately define me.

My mom came back later that night, but my dad never did.

Jack Gartner had gotten on route 160, heading west to California. But he never made it out of Nevada. His car was found at the bottom of a ravine, below what the officers who came to our door to break the news termed *a treacherous curve.*

Killed on impact, we were told.

Did he lose control, or drive off the road on

purpose? Maybe his plan all along had been to leave us and start a new life in California. That's what my mom believed at the time. Still does, in fact.

I, however, am not so sure. My father didn't pack a thing. Sixty dollars and a cancelled credit card, that's all he had on him. I think my dad just gave up. He quit on us, and that was the way he chose to end it. My mom can delude herself all she wants, but I know in my heart that I'm the one who's got it right.

Anyway, the bank took the house soon after my father's death. My mom sold off what little was left. For awhile, we became nomads in the desert. We lived in the only big-ticket item that hadn't been repossessed, a white minivan. The Honda Odyssey was home... until Mom won enough money gambling to move us into a cheap apartment. Our new residence was a dump, but at least it had running water. And it was furnished. Kind of.

When we first stepped across the threshold and Mom caught me scowling at the rusty fixtures, the water-stained ceiling, the musty olive-green carpeting, she tried hard to convince me our new place had its good points.

"Like what?" I asked.

"It's close to The Strip. That'll be convenient."

"Convenient for who?" I sniped. "You?"

"Chase," she said pointedly, "it's better than living in a minivan."

She had a point there, so we moved in the next day. Will's first reaction was to run straight to one of the two back bedrooms and hang up his tattered *twee house* sketch. I followed him and watched as he stood on a soiled mattress on the floor — in a shoebox of a room we were going to have to share — and pinned hope on a wall.

After we were settled, time, as it does, marched on. Will and I attended school, while my mom — still fevered and sick with the gambling virus — spent her days in the casinos.

I turned eighteen that April. But no one really noticed. Well, Will did. Not much got by that kid.

He stuck a candle he found in the back of a drawer in the kitchen on a stale snack cake. He made me sit on the only kitchen chair that didn't rock when you shifted, and then he placed the snack cake on a card table we used as a kitchen table.

Will sang me the most beautiful off-key and from-the-heart rendition of "Happy Birthday" that I have ever heard, before or since. When he was done, I leaned forward to blow out the candle. Will stopped me and told me to make a wish first, so I did. And then I blew out the candle. Will clapped and cheered.

He asked me what I wished for and I told him it was a secret. I didn't want to tell him I wished for him to be given a better life than what we were, at the time, living. My brother and I split the snack cake in two, dinner for the night, and ate in contemplative silence.

Summer arrived that year and I somehow managed to graduate. But—with my trust fund long gone—college was no longer on the table. With no real guidance, and a lot of pent-up frustration, my downward slide took hold. I was angry all the time, and ended up getting into too many fights to count. The places in Vegas where I'd started hanging were tough. Early on, I got my ass kicked…often.

But then something happened.

I learned how to use my strength, my quickness, *and* my anger. I started to win. I had a real knack for fighting and rapidly turned into a badass nobody messed with. I earned street cred. All that really meant was guys started showing me respect and girls suddenly wanted to have sex with me. I happily obliged more than a few of the latter.

But all that shit meant nothing, I was empty inside. I had no one to talk to about the mixed-up emotions I didn't know how to deal with. Like, why was I so angry all the time? Why did I like to fight so much? Why did it feel so good to make someone else hurt?

But mostly I wondered why I missed my dad so much.

I missed talking to my father, seeing his face everyday. I had relied on him, I still needed him. But he was gone. He took his own life. Why couldn't I just accept what had happened and forget him?

But I couldn't, and, worse yet, I longed for answers.

Every day, for a while, in my quest for enlightenment, I'd grab the bus outside our apartment and visit my father. Well, I'd visit his grave. At the head of where my father rested eternally, I'd sit under a big stone angel kneeling by his grave — thankful for the little bit of shade she offered under the hot, beating sun of the desert.

Sweaty and lost, I'd ask her if she could tell me why my dad wasn't still alive. Why had God allowed Dad to take himself away? Why did my father choose to leave me? Why would he leave Mom and Will too? Was our love not enough for him? Did he regret his decision when he realized there was no going back?

Of course, the stone angel had no answers, and one day I just quit going. No more sitting in the shadow of the angel, no more hot and beating sun. No more asking questions that could never be answered.

My trips to the cemetery were over, but that didn't mean I wanted to forget that *someone* — even though he'd left—had once believed in me. Despite everything, I still loved my father and part of me yearned to be just like him.

So, July of that year, I had his angel's likeness—the stone one at his grave—inked in profile on the middle of my upper back, between my shoulder blades.

I shift in the passenger seat now.

I can almost feel her back there, watching over me, like my dad's angel watches over him. And like his angel, mine is kneeling. The edges of her heavy robe lie in a puddle of fabric around her. Her wings are folded against her back. Her hair is long, obscuring the side of her face. And her head is bowed. In supplication or in shame, I haven't decided which. But if she's been watching the shit I've been doing these past two years, it's probably in shame.

After the angel tat healed, Mom hit for more money. I successfully talked her into paying for another tattoo, guilted her into it really. In any case, I ended up with big, intricately detailed wings inked up and over my shoulder blades. The top feathers curve onto my shoulders, while the wings dip down the sides of my back, effectively framing the angel.

But the angel and the wings weren't enough. I wanted something more to remember my father, something to remind me always of that final night, when it was just him and me, eating Chinese food on the floor of an empty home, a last supper shared.

I kept coming back to the cookie, the fortune inside, the hope it symbolized.

As I stand before you, judge me not.

Words printed on a piece of paper, but really they were so much more. So I had those words inked — in concise and script letters — around my left bicep.

My tats were but temporal attempts to heal my soul, as my heart remained an open wound. There was no solace to be had at home. In fact, things were getting worse. I started to drink and do drugs to ease the pain and fill the void. I hated what had happened to our family. Seeing Will transformed from an energetic little boy to a sullen nine-year-old left me sad and frustrated. And watching my mother try to heal her fractured heart with gambling — and eventually men — just pissed me the fuck off.

But at least Mom wasn't indulging in one-night stands like I'd been doing. Nope, Abby actually went out on dates. Still, her attempt at dating led to a revolving door of boyfriends. Some lasted a week or two, some a little longer, but the one common denominator they all shared was that not a single one liked me.

Mom told me to try harder, give these guys a

chance for her sake. I laughed and told Abby her men could blow me. "Chase, don't be crude," was her response.

By the end of the summer Mom hooked up with what turned out to be steady boyfriend number three. I was no fool; I immediately sensed my days were numbered. I would've had to have been blind not to see the writing on the wall, a wall I didn't realize I was hurtling toward. But it wasn't just Abby's lame new boyfriend disliking me that was a problem. There was something else, something she'd never admit to. There was no escaping it though, not really.

I saw Abby's problem every day when I looked in the mirror.

Standing in a cramped and steam-filled bathroom, hot water running, can of shave cream poised in hand, I couldn't deny the truth in front of me. I'd swipe at the misted mirror with my free hand, leaving it streaky, but mostly clear. And it wasn't me I saw in the reflection, it was my father. That's how much I looked like Jack Gartner, even at eighteen. And *that* was my mother's real problem.

Shit. Even thinking about it now—two years later—fucks with my head.

I glance over at Tate. He's quiet, taking long pulls from the bottle. I shift in my seat and wind up the window the rest of the way. Time to assess my bleary reflection, time to compare it to what it was, time to compare it to the man who made me…I sometimes do this just to fuck with myself.

When I take in my reflection, I laugh. Hell, the resemblance is still uncanny. And just like when I used to stare at the steamed-up mirror in the bathroom, it's my dad's eyes staring back at me now. But these pale blues are all mine. Yeah, *his* whites were never shot with red like mine.

Still, even with the bloodshot eyes, similarities far outweigh differences. Though it's not *short and tidy* — like Grandma Gartner would like it to be — my hair is the exact same shade as her son's once was, light brown. Jack also blessed me with his straight nose, his square jaw, and his defined cheekbones. Everyone used to say my dad was good-looking, I guess I am too. Girls seem to think so, that's for sure. And my mother sure was smitten with my dad.

Abby used to lean across the front seat of the sporty car my dad bought for himself during the good times. Will and I would be in the back, rolling our eyes at each other. My mom would kiss my dad, making him swerve a little as he drove. She'd tell him he was gorgeous, and that she loved him. Dad would laugh and tell Abby he loved her even more. He'd say his love for her burned hotter than the Vegas sun above us. My mom loved that shit. Will and I, however, would groan in disgust and make gagging noises.

Shit, I feel like gagging now. Not because of the memory, but at how closely I still resemble my dead father. I turn away from my reflection. I can't bear to endure this self-inflicted torture any longer. No wonder I was fucking sent away. Too bad I couldn't disappear completely just as easily right now. Guess, in a way, that's why I live my life the way I do, filling it with drugs...sex...violence.

Back then my very presence in my mom's life must have been a constant reminder of all she had lost. When you're striving to move on, you don't need an anchor to the past. She could move forward with Will, he was just a kid. Besides, he looked like her, not like my father. But I was eighteen, an adult, and far too much my father's son for everyone's comfort. I guess it was just too difficult for Mom to look at me — see *him* — and be reminded of all she'd once had.

So the day steady boyfriend number three, a guy named Gary, told her she could move in with him, I kind of fucking knew the invitation wouldn't be extended to me.

Sure enough, on a blistering hot afternoon, my

mom sent Will out to ride his bike and told me we had to talk. She sat me down on the ratty couch in our shitty apartment. I felt like a condemned man waiting to hear his fate, and all the while the noisy air conditioning unit in the window behind me kept blowing gusts of lukewarm air across the back of my neck.

Not that it mattered. I barely noticed. I was mostly numb. In preparation for this "talk," I'd done a couple of lines of coke in my room. Of course, I hadn't brought that shit out until after Will had left. One thing I stuck to was that I never let my little brother see me taking part in any of my newfound vices.

Anyway, that day in the living room, I couldn't sit still. Fidgeting, fidgeting, tapping my foot. Mom took no notice, she was almost as bad. Pacing back and forth in front of me, smoking a cigarette, a new habit she'd just acquired. Gary smoked, so she'd picked up the habit too. *Pathetic*, I remember thinking.

My mother appeared so edgy and wired I almost asked her if she was dabbling in drugs, like me, or if what she had to say was really just that fucking bad. She started speaking before I ever got the chance.

"You're not a kid anymore, Chase," she began, still pacing, ashes peppering the olive-green carpeting.

She took a drag, crinkled her brow, and leaned

over to stub her cigarette out in a plastic ashtray on a low table.

"You have to get started on doing something, somewhere, kid," she said as she spun to face me.

She stood right in front of me, and though my head was down I watched her every move. She blew out a breath and I watched her dark blonde bangs lift up off her forehead. A few strands stuck to her skin. Mom was starting to sweat.

"So, Grandma Gartner called the other day," she continued, her words deliberate, pointed, like a knife. "She said she's got lots of room in that old farmhouse back in Ohio. And she sure could use some company."

I looked up at her in disbelief. This woman who'd given me life tried to smile, but she could not. She knew damn well she was spewing pure bullshit. She just wanted rid of me.

"Just spit it out," I ground through clenched teeth, my voice far from even.

"Okay, of course, honey." She looked everywhere but at me. "Uh, so, Gram thinks moving back to Harmony Creek might do you some good, get you out of Vegas, give you a chance to start over, and —"

"Mom, I'm only eighteen. Start over?" I blew out a quick breath. "I haven't even had a chance to get started *here*."

Her expression grew stern. "Chase, don't act like I don't know the things you do behind my back." I tried to protest, but she shushed me. "I know you use drugs. I know you bring girls back when Will's not around. That shit isn't going to fly once we move in with Gary. He won't stand for it, Chase. He has standards—"

I snorted, "The fuck he does—"

"I'm not going to argue with you about it," she said, her voice tired and cracking.

When she reached for her pack of cigarettes, I noticed her hands were shaking. "Honey, I just think Grandma Gartner's is the best place for you right now, okay?"

I picked at a hole in my jeans. "Do I have a choice?" I asked, defeated, and, truthfully, feeling like I'd just been set adrift.

She shook her head no.

I'd known it was coming, but her words still flayed me up the middle and pierced my already damaged heart. I was shocked that my heart could continue beating, since it felt all smashed to hell. But beat it did. In fact, my heart pumped faster and faster, like it was going to burst right out of my fucking chest. Whether my reaction was from cocaine...or despair...I couldn't quite figure.

With my heart pounding like a sped-up death knell, I tried to push some words out of my cotton-dry mouth. "Mom…" I croaked, my voice catching.

I just couldn't finish.

Verbal communication failed me, so I tried to meet her eyes, speak to her soul. Was this really what she wanted? Send her eldest son away? Give up on me? Just like Dad did with all of us.

I searched and searched, but my mother had no answers in her big green eyes, no more than the stone angel had at my father's grave.

Abby took in a stuttered breath and turned away. She swiped at a tear. "It's for the best, Chase," she mumbled.

And then she left me sitting there, all alone, warm air blowing across the back of my neck.

I went back to my room and cut up three more lines.

That was nearly two years ago and here I am. Mom is still in Las Vegas with Will, on steady boyfriend number six, last I heard. She's still chasing the elusive jackpot too, hoping to recapture the life she once knew.

Good luck with that, I think bitterly. *Jackpot, my ass.* If anyone needs to hit a fucking jackpot, it's me.

Suddenly, drug-induced visions of flashing pots

of gold swim lazily into my head, along with some break-dancing leprechauns, and I can't help but chuckle.

Tate looks over. He must think my mood has improved, 'cause he starts talking all excitedly about how much money we're going to make from our new business venture with Kyle. I listen to his voice, not really hearing any words, but then the cell buzzes and I am alert, very alert.

Tate tosses it my way. "That there would be the ladies," he says — all smooth like — as I catch the cell with one hand. Even impaired, my coordination is impeccable.

"Ladies, my ass." I roll my eyes.

Tate laughs, knowing as well as I do that the two girls we're meeting up with tonight are no ladies. They're looking for the same thing we are, but therein lies the beauty.

"What's it say?" he asks, nodding to the cell.

The text is kind of blurry, but, then again, everything is. I blink a few times and my vision clears. When I read it out loud, I mimic a high-pitched girl's voice, just to be an ass. "Crystal and I are almost at the lake. Come prepared. Tammy. Laugh out loud, winking smiley face."

"Dude-e-e." Tate shoots me a knowing sidelong

glance. "You know what *come prepared* means, right? You got that covered, yeah?"

As reckless as I am—and that's pretty fucking reckless—I always make sure I wrap my shit up. Better safe than sorry. But as I feel around in the pockets of my jeans I realize I've left the condoms at home. "Fuck," I mutter.

The blue *Welcome to Pennsylvania* sign looms ahead, our headlights flashing off the reflective letters.

Tate asks, "What?"

I rake my fingers through my hair. "I forgot the goddamn things at home."

"Not a problem. We'll just stop at the convenience store across the state line."

"Bad idea," I counter. "Cops are always hanging out in there. You think they won't notice how fucked up we are?"

"How fucked up *you* are," Tate corrects, laughing. "I didn't smoke nearly as much as you."

"You smoked plenty," I mumble under my breath.

But Tate is right, I smoked more. And Tate smoked only weed. Plus, my friend didn't see the pills Kyle slipped me before we left.

Still, I nod to the almost-empty bottle. "You pretty much drank that whole thing, dickhead. You'll never pass a field sobriety test."

"Yeah, but I don't plan on taking one, my friend. And, I hide it better than you." He shrugs. "Trust me, I got it covered. Just wait in the car. It'll only take a sec."

Tate's always confident like this. He can talk anyone into just about anything. I always tell him he's a natural-born salesman. Maybe if we ever get our shit together he can do something legit using his smooth ways. It's cool, it's Tate's thing, and it helps make him popular. He's an okay-looking guy—brown hair, brown eyes, kind of skinny—but it's his smooth talk that gets him in with the girls. They eat that shit up.

We cross the state line, turn into the convenience store. No cop cars. "See, we're good," Tate says, still as confident as ever.

I flip up my black hoodie hood and slouch down in my seat. "Just be quick," I mumble.

Tate hesitates, and I know something is up. "What the fuck are you waiting for?" I ask.

He begins his sentence with "Don't be pissed—" and I cut him off right away, hoping I won't have to kick my good friend's skinny ass. It would be a damn shame really, since Tate wouldn't stand a chance against the likes of me. I am way bigger and far stronger, and the rage within me has no match.

"What?" I spit out, clenching my jaw.

Tate ignores my attitude; he's used to it. "I kind of need you to hold on to something while I go in there. Just in case."

"Just in case of what?"

I am running out of patience. I scrub my hand down my face, wary to hear what Tate the salesman is up to now.

He smirks, and I tell him to knock that shit off, save it for the "ladies."

"Okay, okay." He raises his hands in mock surrender. "I may have kind of asked Kyle to give us a little something to get our entrepreneurial gig started."

"Us?" I say, feeling the anger rise up. "You didn't even know I was going to sell with you until about ten minutes ago."

"What can I say, man." Tate places his hand over his heart. "I had faith."

"Whatever."

I try to stay pissed, because what he did was really out of line, but my anger fades fast. High as I am, these strong emotions are too fucking slippery to hold on to for very long.

Tate hands me a plastic packet filled with little pills, a rainbow of color. "Jesus." I know all too well exactly what this shit is. "X? You're fucking higher than I thought. We're supposed to start small, bitch. Move a little bud, see how it goes."

Tate shrugs. "We'll make more money this way. Like, I know we can sell to the girls tonight. Hell, I bet we can talk them into buying *our* hits."

He's laughing at his own ingenuity, but I ignore him. I'm too busy trying to count the pills in the packet. But being in the condition I am in, it's a bit of a challenge.

"How much is this anyway?" I ask, giving up on figuring it out for myself.

"Twenty hits," he tells me, and then he has the balls to throw another packet in my lap. "Make that forty…maybe a little more."

"You're fucking crazy. If we get caught, Tate, this isn't possession. This is possession with intent to sell."

"That's why I'm leaving the shit here with you."

"Oh, that's real fucking cool." Back to being pissed, even my high can't calm me now. I whip one of the packets back at Tate. "I am so not getting caught with forty hits of Ecstasy, asshole."

"Calm down, man." He gingerly picks up the packet I've just thrown and holds it out for me to take back. "If a cop shows up just hit the road."

"What about you?" I ask as I grudgingly accept

the X.

Tate grins. "Don't worry about me. You know I can play it cool. Just swing by after the heat's gone, and we'll be back in business."

"The heat? What is this, the seventies?" I ask, laughing, but Tate's already out the door.

I tuck the two packets of Ecstasy into the back pocket of my jeans and think nothing more of it. Until a few short minutes later when a state cop pulls into the lot. Then, I panic.

I start climbing over the console to get the fuck out of there, but, suddenly, with every fiber of my being, I know I've just made the dumbest mistake of my life. That, however, doesn't stop me from slipping down into the driver's seat, throwing the car into reverse. I hit the gas, peel out of the parking lot, and leave a cloud of gravel and dust in my wake.

I've got the Focus up to eighty, music playing… loud, loud, fucking blaring. Maybe I can outrun this cocksucker? I'm tapping my hands on the steering wheel along with the beat, flying so fast it's amazing I don't lose control and crash.

But I don't, I stay steady.

I even make it a good five miles down the road before a cop heading my way—backup, I'm sure— screeches to a wide arced stop in front of me. His patrol car blocks the entire road, so I have no choice but to hit the brakes and squeal to a halt.

My car ends up parallel to the cop car, both of us straddling the lanes, engines idling like we're in some fucking action movie. The air reeks of burning rubber, and smoke billows around us. The speakers beat out a song from 50 Cent that is frankly ironic at this point.

When all the smoke clears, the sign for the lake is right smack dab in front of me. I can't help but laugh. The shit situation I'm in, and all I can think of is that Crystal and Tammy are out there, waiting, for two boys who are never going to show.

Two more cops—including the one from the store—pull up behind me. I pitch the door open, tumble from the seat. I hit the warm pavement and try to stand. Someone yells, "Hold it right there, hands on your head."

I hear guns being drawn, cocked. This isn't a movie, I know they're loaded. I squint to try to see what's happening, but all the flashing lights leave me blinded. Before I can think another drug-muddled thought, someone tackles me from behind. My face smacks right into the yellow center line, but I don't feel a fucking thing.

Whoever tackles me yanks down my hood, frisks me, and comes up with my wallet. Oh, and the forty hits of X, of course.

It's all ambient noise from that point on, but I do hear, "Chase Gartner, you're under arrest."

I have no idea that, despite the altered state I'm in, these will be the last coherent words I will remember for a very long time.

The time following has no sense of structure. Days, weeks, they all blend together. I'm in jail, facing a long, long list of charges. But it's the X that has me fucked.

Bond is set high. I call my mom, but all she does is cry. Like, these horrible wailing sobs that do nothing but make my head ache more than ever. She keeps apologizing for not having the money and swears she'll help me when she can. I hang up. I won't be holding my breath. The past has taught me not to put too much stock into Abby's flimsy promises. Mirages in the desert are what they are—get too close and they disappear.

My grandmother wants to mortgage the farmhouse, all the property around it. We're talking a good fifty-five acres. It'd be enough to make bail, but I tell her *no way*. She's done enough for me already, and look at how I've repaid her. I don't deserve her money...or her love.

So I'm on my own. And not thinking very clearly. Once all the illegal shit is out of my system, I find myself in a constant state of agitation. I can't sleep, I barely eat. I sweat bullets even when it feels like I'm freezing.

Eventually all that passes, but then all I want to do is fight. Like beat heads in. It's worse than when I was back in Vegas; I feel so much more fucking rage. I sit around clenching my fists, hoping for a chance to kick some poor unsuspecting soul's ass.

Finally, my wish is granted.

They throw a cellmate in with me and my ass is on him like an animal, beating the hell out of this never-saw-me-coming sap. But then two guards see what I'm doing, pull me off the bloodied and broken man, and promptly return the favor.

Another blur of pain.

This one, though, I welcome. The medical staff gives me plenty of drugs, legal ones this time. And still more before I am put before the judge.

Even in the sedated fog I float around in, I quickly learn the law...and some new math.

MDMA, Ecstasy—X, as I like to call it—is a schedule I narcotic, and carries as stiff a penalty as heroin if you're caught dealing, which they naturally assume I was. Casual users don't tote around forty-plus hits of Ecstasy, but dealers do.

I say nothing one way or the other to dispel their myth, I rat no one out. I just stay quiet and accept my fate.

My math lesson continues...

Ten pills are equal to one gram, and I've been caught with over forty pills. Forty pills equal four grams, which is more than enough to be charged with possession with intent to sell. But I already knew that part, right?

My lesson isn't over though. It's only just beginning.

I learn in Pennsylvania, the state in which I've been apprehended, four grams can easily earn you a prison sentence. This is especially true when you don't have enough money to hire a good attorney. Add to that, your public defender isn't getting paid enough to care. Not that you're doing much to help the overworked, underpaid man do his job. And, oh yeah, don't forget that one prior arrest for fighting last fall. It didn't seem like much at the time, but it sure haunts your ass now.

Are you keeping up?

Some final math...

Four grams buys you a six-year sentence at a state correctional institute when you have no resources, and, really, no heart to fight it.

Twenty years of age feels like ninety when your freedom is stripped away.

It takes one hundred and forty-three steps to walk down a long, noisy corridor to reach cell block seventy-two.

And when they turn the key, you hear one life — the only one you've ever known up until now — ending.

"It's all about the numbers, man," as Tate would say.

It sure is, my friend. It sure is.

Continue the story...

Available on Amazon, Barnes & Noble, and ITunes

Read the first chapter of *Harbour Falls*

HARBOUR FALLS

Chapter 1

Sitting in the idling car in the deserted and rain-drenched parking lot on tiny Cove Beach in Harbour Falls, I absently turned a business card over and over in my hands. Fingertips over smooth, heavy cardstock, with raised, royal-blue printing on one side...

Harbour Falls Realtors
Northern Maine Coastal Properties
Ami Dubois-Hensley
Agent

With an edge of a fingernail free of polish, I traced the outline of the design. It was meant to be a representation of my destination today: a mass of land out there in the churning waters bearing the ominous name of Fade Island. Heavy fogs, quite common in this tucked-away corner of northern Maine, often swallowed up the island—giving the illusion of it "fading" into the sea.

Suddenly the rain intensified without warning. Sheeting off the windshield in thick bands of water, my view of the ink-colored waves crashing along the beach blurred. I leaned forward to turn the wiper control up a notch and caught my refection in the rearview mirror. Wow, this perpetual dampness was really wreaking havoc on my long hair. I smoothed the unruly strands back into place as best as I could and noticed the California sun-kissed highlights, always so evident in my natural honey-brown shade, were already fading. Just like the island in the fog.

I'd only been back a few days, but life as I knew it felt slippery, like it could get away from me if I let my guard down. I adjusted the mirror; uncertainty warred with determination in the hazel eyes — so like my father's — staring back at me. Questions that had haunted me since I'd first decided to return home washed over me anew. *Why had I really come back to Harbour Falls? Just how dangerous could it end up being? Should I turn around and go back…before it turned out to be too late?*

But it was too late. A white SUV had just pulled to a stop and parked in the space to the right of my car. Ami Dubois — or rather Ami Dubois-*Hensley* — opened the driver's side door. As she began to fumble with one of those oversized golf umbrellas, it was clear, despite her seated position and long raincoat, that she was very pregnant. Guess she and Sean Hensley, friends of mine from the past, had decided it was finally time to start a family. Truthfully, it surprised me they'd waited this long.

Five years had passed since I'd last seen Sean and Ami, having attended their wedding in Harbour Falls. At the time we'd all been twenty-two years old and freshly graduated from college—me from Yale, and Sean and Ami from the University of Maine.

How time flew.

A twinge of sorrow tugged at my heart as I recalled how their wedding was the first major event I'd attended with Julian, a man with whom I ended up spending six years of my life. Of course we'd just been starting out back then. And now it was all over. Back in May we'd decided to go our separate ways. People change over time, sometimes drifting in different directions without ever realizing it. Until it's too late.

Ami's sudden rap on my driver's side window tore me from my ruminations. I yanked at the belt of the black trench coat I was wearing, tightening it, as the thin material of the wrap dress I wore underneath would offer little respite from the cold and rain.

I opened the car door, and Ami, stepping back, smiled warmly and tilted the umbrella so I could slip underneath it. "Maddy, it's been too long. God, how have you been?"

"Good," I replied. "Just trying to adjust to this weather."

Her pale blue eyes scanned down my form. "Well, you look *amazing*. I was so excited when Mayor Fitch…uh, I mean, your dad called and said you were moving back."

Somehow balancing the umbrella in such a way as to keep us dry, she pulled me in for an awkward one-armed hug. Her swollen tummy pressed against my slender frame for a moment, until she drew away.

"It's great to see you too," I said. "But I'm not moving back permanently, you know. It's just for a few months." To keep the conversation from delving into exactly *why* I was back for such a specific amount of time, I motioned to her stomach. "Congratulations, by the way. My dad didn't say anything about—"

"Oh, Maddy, I am *so* excited," Ami interrupted. "Only one more month."

She rubbed her stomach, her hand gliding over the big, clear buttons on her powder-blue raincoat. Standing there—ash-blond hair cascading down her shoulders in big, bouncy curls and a smile as vibrant as ever—Ami radiated happiness.

I'd forgotten how pretty she was, and pregnancy certainly agreed with her. Truly pleased for my once dear friend, I said, "How's Sean? Thrilled, I bet."

"*Very.*"

"Do you know if you're having a boy or a girl?"

"Um, no." Ami hesitated and pressed her lips together. She took an inordinate amount of time to adjust the umbrella to block the swirling winds that were starting to kick up all around us, and added flatly, "We'd rather be surprised."

"Oh," I said slowly, "OK."

An awkward silence ensued, and we both watched as a fast-food wrapper of some sort blew by us. It adhered to the trunk of my car, and Ami reached to snatch it up. "Nice car," she murmured, crumpling the wrapper in her palm and dragging a finger through the beading raindrops. "Sean would love a BMW."

There was something in her tone, something that made me feel self-conscious. Being a best-selling author of several novels allowed me to enjoy perks, such as my burgundy M6, back in Los Angeles. Flashy sports cars were a dime a dozen in California. But I'd forgotten, the people from this part of my life remembered me best as quiet, unassuming Madeleine Fitch—daughter of beloved and low-key widower, Mayor William V. Fitch.

"Thanks," I mumbled as I shifted away, shivering

as icy raindrops began to pelt the back of my head.

Ami stuffed the crumpled wrapper in her raincoat pocket and said, "Uh, we should start over to the ferry. Jennifer is expecting us by two." And just like that, everything was back to normal.

Jennifer Weston and her cousin, Brody, owned the only two passenger ferries that operated out of Cove Beach. During the summer, in addition to the usual service, the Westons offered whale-watching excursions, usually for tourists passing through on the much less-traveled route to Canada. Or sometimes folks would venture up from Bar Harbor to explore this quiet little area, since it was relatively close. Not to mention somewhat infamous. But now that we were well into September, there'd be no whale watchers, no curiosity seekers. The ferries would be used strictly as transportation between Harbour Falls and my destination today, Fade Island.

A rocky and rugged landmass, mostly covered in thick, impenetrable forests, the island was located several miles from the mainland. While the eastern half remained untouched wilderness, the western half had seen its share of development over the years. Long ago a tiny fishing village had sprung up near the docks, and several Cotswold-style cottages were built to house the fishermen and their families.

Over time those early settlers dispersed, and the state had the cottages converted into rental properties. When I was growing up in Harbour Falls, it was not uncommon for families to spend at least a part of their summer vacation over on Fade Island. But I'd never been there. Not once. Eventually, as the residents of Harbour Falls expanded their vacation horizons, fewer and fewer people came to the island, and the cottages soon fell into disrepair.

But all that changed a few years back when the state of Maine sold the island to a private party. Almost immediately money poured in. The little fishing town was renovated, giving it a quirky, art deco uplift. The rental cottages were refurbished and made modern but in such a way as to retain their charm.

And a former resident of Harbour Falls—a man named Adam Ward—had a huge home in the style of Frank Lloyd Wright built overlooking the sea on the northern end of the island. Really it was more like a compound, complete with a private dock, a set of garages, even an airfield. It was hard to believe I'd once gone to school with the guy.

I had searched and searched to see if Adam had been the person who'd bought the island. It made sense, with the fancy home and all. But I came up empty-handed. The real estate transaction I culled from public records listed only a limited liability company with a bogus name as the owner. And the bogus name led me back to Harbour Falls Realtors but not to Adam. So the owner wished to remain anonymous. That was fine with me. I was tired of running around in circles.

One thing I knew for certain: Ami, as an agent of Harbour Falls Realtors, handled the business of renting out the cottages to a now-steady stream of wealthy summer vacationers looking for a private retreat. But Ami had no idea, in my case, she was about to rent to someone with a secret reason for wanting to stay on Fade Island.

It wasn't the peace and solitude touted in the online brochure that I sought. Nor did I have a desire to just hang out in a nicely renovated cottage. Not even that picturesque lighthouse depicted on Ami's business card, and located on the far southeastern tip of the island, held any appeal. Many a painter and photographer had traveled to the island to capture the image of the tall, imposing structure that harkened back to days past. Positioned at the end of a rocky peninsula and standing sentry in the shadow of a curved shelf of steep, jutting cliffs, the lighthouse was an artist's dream, even if it was no longer in use. But I wasn't here for that either.

No, I was much more intrigued by something the brochure failed to mention: the huge, private estate overlooking the sea on the *other* end of the island. To be more precise, I was intrigued by the sole occupant of that estate, the former Harbour Falls resident, Adam Ward. In fact, I'd purposely chosen the cottage closest to his home as the one I wished to view.

My father told Ami I needed a quiet place to work through a bad case of writer's block. But that was far from the truth. Only he—and my agent, Katie—knew the real reason behind my wanting to spend these autumn months on a lonely, isolated island. It had *everything* to do with researching the subject matter for my next book and absolutely nothing to do with some silly, made-up case of writer's block.

And my research had begun before I'd even arrived. For example, I knew there were only four year-round residents on Fade Island, as it was not the most hospitable place once the summer faded into fall. Heavy rains and storms were common throughout most of the year, but things became particularly treacherous during the winter months.

Snowstorms and loss of power were not uncommon. And there was no reliable way to get off the island, except for the ferry. But the ferry didn't run when the weather got too crazy. Nothing did, not even the alternative means of transportation — several boats and a corporate jet — that Mr. Ward often employed. During those times Fade Island lived up to its name in another way; it was as if it faded from civilization.

The rain slowed to a fine mist as we approached the ferry, and Ami lowered the umbrella. "So who can I expect to see once we get over there?" I asked and then added, "Like, who lives out there year-round?"

Obviously I was well aware of the identities of the full-time residents. I thought I was being clever, feigning ignorance for Ami's benefit. The less she knew *I* knew, the more likely she'd not question my cover story. Right? Maybe not.

I took one look at her face and wished I'd kept my mouth shut. "You don't know? You've never heard?" She eyed me skeptically. "Surely, your father told you."

I shook my head and looked away. A slender, pale girl with dark hair was messing with some ropes aboard the ferry, so I pretended to be focused on her.

But when I tried to keep on walking, Ami stopped and grabbed my arm. I couldn't meet her gaze, certain she'd catch on to my deception. "Madeleine! You *have* to know Adam Ward lives on the island. It's no secret he moved out there after..." She lowered her voice.

"Well, after what happened."

She was right; it was no secret. Back when Adam lived in Harbour Falls, he had everything, the world at his feet. A brilliant mind, he excelled in all things academic. But software engineering was his specialty. He coded and developed elaborate software systems that had every college and university with a computer engineering program vying for his commitment to study at their institution. And since his academic abilities were rivaled only by his athletic prowess, those schools with a football program offered Adam everything they could without attracting the attention of the NCAA. In the end, though, he gave up football and enrolled at MIT.

All those things were impressive, but what had caught my attention back then were his striking good looks. He was tall and had an amazing body, gorgeous jet-black hair, and stunning blue eyes. Yeah, it had been hard not to notice him. And notice him I did. But, sadly, he never seemed to look my way.

"Maddyyyy! Earth to Maddy." Ami waved her hand in front of my face.

"Oh, sorry. I was just…I was just remembering," I stammered, "um, high school."

Ami had once been one of my best friends, and surely she recalled my unrequited interest in Mr.

Ward. As if on cue, she smiled knowingly and said, "In case you were maybe wondering, he *is* still single."

I barked out a nervous laugh. "We're not in high school, Ami. I think my crushing days are behind me. Besides…" I trailed off.

She knew why. After all, everyone had heard the rumors.

"They're just unfounded accusations and idle gossip," Ami said in a hushed voice, her defense of Adam surprisingly fervent. "You know that, right?"

"It's really not that." And it wasn't, but I didn't want to explain myself to Ami. "It's just…" I fumbled for an explanation. "I didn't come here to start something with Adam Ward, OK?" *Small lie.*

Ami cast a doubtful glance my way, but before she could persist in her matchmaking attempt, I pointed to the ferry and said, "It's after two. We'd better get going."

The half-hour ride through the choppy waters to Fade Island was mostly silent, Ami and I lost in our own thoughts. Jennifer Weston, the slender, pale girl who'd been messing with the ropes, didn't say anything more to us than she absolutely had to. A number of times when I glanced over at the ferry pilot's house, I caught her glaring at me. But I had no idea why.

Before today I'd never had contact with her. She'd gone to school at Harbour Falls High but graduated a few years before me. Still, I knew who she was. How could I not? Jennifer had been married for two years to my other best friend back in high school, J.T. O'Brien. I hadn't kept in touch with J.T. after leaving Harbour Falls, but I heard a lot about him from my dad. And what he told me wasn't good.

A few years back, J.T. had gotten into trouble with the law — some kind of drug and alcohol charge. After a stint in rehab, he surprised everyone by marrying Jennifer. She'd always had a thing for J.T., but he'd never shown any interest in her. So when they ran off to Vegas for a quickie wedding, nobody could figure out why. My father said there was speculation that she'd gotten knocked up. But nine months came… and went…with no baby.

All of this occurred during the spring and summer before my final year at Yale. At the time I was interning at a publishing house in New York, so I didn't pay too much attention to the updates from home. When I returned to college that fall, I met Julian. And once we were together, I hardly kept up with the Harbour Falls gossip. Following a quick visit back for Ami and Sean's wedding the following summer, Julian and I moved to Los Angeles. I embarked on my writing career, and soon my life was too busy to worry about people from my past. Except for the occasional, short holiday visit home, this whole area had fallen off my radar completely.

Well, maybe not *completely*.

There was one huge Harbour Falls Mystery — as the press had dubbed it — I could not avoid hearing about. The story even dominated the national news for a time. And inevitably, mostly on book tours and during interviews, I was asked for *my* thoughts regarding the case. I imagined people were curious for two reasons. One, I was from Harbour Falls, a primary location involved in the mystery. And two, I was a crime and mystery novelist, and the facts of the case mirrored the kinds of things I wrote about.

Only my cases were purely fictional, so my standard response had always been the same: *I have no interest in real-life cases.* And that had been true. But it no longer was; things were about to change.

The Harbour Falls Mystery was the real reason I was here. I had every intention of basing my next novel on the facts of the case. I was tired of fiction; I wanted to write a true crime novel. Plus there was a little part of me — the detective that lurks in all of us — that dreamed of *solving* this case.

But nobody knew that this case held more than

a professional interest for me. Not because the main locale was Harbour Falls, and not because the mystery involved the disappearance of a local I'd once known. And, truth be told, had once envied. Nor was it the fact that this local, Chelsea Hannigan, had gone missing the night before her wedding. Scandalous, though it was.

What piqued my curiosity was the man Chelsea had been on the verge of marrying—Adam Ward. He was the man at the center of the mystery. He was the man whose life had been altered when Chelsea disappeared, after he was named as the number one suspect.

What role, if any, had he played in her disappearance? Though never formally charged, many believed he was far from innocent.

Well I was here to uncover the truth. There was just one small problem.

Contrary to what I'd told Ami, I *was* interested in Adam Ward. Still. Despite how ridiculous I knew it was, I couldn't wait to run into Adam. Would he even remember me? Maybe not. But I wasn't the shy girl I'd been back then.

Of course I was playing with fire. If he ever suspected I was investigating him in order to research my new novel, he'd hardly be pleased. I might even see firsthand just how supposedly dangerous he could be.

At the thought, a little shudder ran through me. Whether it was due to fear, excitement, or both, I wasn't sure. I knew I should analyze it and get my head straight before I ended up in trouble.

But I'd run out of time. Because the fog began to lift, and in the distance, Fade Island came into view.

Continue the story…

Available on Amazon, Barnes & Noble, ITunes, and Kobo